FIRST MATE'S
ACCIDENTAL WIFE

IN THE STARS ROMANCE: GYPSY MOTH 1

EVE LANGLAIS

Copyright © 2017, Eve Langlais

Cover Art by Dreams 2 Media © 2017

Produced in Canada

Published by Eve Langlais

http://www.EveLanglais.com

E-ISBN-13: 978 1 77384 003 1

PRINT ISBN: 978 1 77384 004 8

CHAPTER 1

"Try not to kill anyone."

Captain Jameson shot him a glare along with the order.

"I'll try and hold off on any murderous sprees, but I can't promise," First Mate Damon Faulkner declared with a grin as they tromped through the tubes connecting the *Gypsy Moth* to the starship they were rendezvousing with in the Lxa Galaxy. The fact that only a flexible tube kept them from the freezing ravages of space was something everyone tried not to dwell on. Accidents were rare. Intentional acts of sabotage, on the other hand...

"We are not here to start a war with the Kanishqui."

"Says the man who is boarding their ship under false pretenses."

"Not entirely false. I do indeed have some business

to discuss with the commander," Captain Jameson said.

"And while you're discussing, I get to kidnap someone." A woman. Not their usual fare. The captain preferred to deal in cargo that stayed in boxes and didn't talk back.

Living creatures tended to cause headaches. Those with speech capabilities usually complained or cried. As for the animals? They shit. All the time. And someone had to clean it.

"The term you're looking for is rescue," the captain corrected. "And so long as we do it without causing any death, I should be able to convince the Kanishqui not to retaliate."

"You mean bribe?"

"If I have to. I came prepared."

"What if I get caught?"

"Then it was nice having you work for me."

As first mate, he was second only to the captain. But as second, he was considered expendable.

"Not exactly reassuring."

"Then don't screw up."

"Since when do we indulge in rescue missions?" Having served with the captain for ten EC years—as in Earth Calendar, the standardized unit of time amongst humans raised in the colonies or the space stations—Damon had never been called upon to save anyone. Thief, spy, assassin—yes—but hero? That was for those galactic cowboys in their shiny ships who got paid in promotions and too few credits for a living.

The captain tossed him a quick glance. "I'm doing this as a favor for a friend."

"Pretty big fucking favor," Damon muttered. "Does the commander we're visiting suspect we're coming to steal his prize?"

"Better hope not or we'll be disintegrated the moment we enter his ship. Now shut it. He's probably listening."

Wouldn't matter if he were. Damon and the captain had engaged their FOZ protocol—which stood for Friends Only Zone. When enabled, they could communicate with each other, but anyone not in the loop would only hear gibberish. No translator available on the market could yet crack the codes the FOZ protocol used—a special invention of their resident geek gal, Einstein. But even she admitted it was only a matter of time before someone developed something to infiltrate it, especially now that she'd sold the patent for a sum that had too many zeros attached. The woman could easily retire and live the life of leisure, so why did Einstein still work?

Who the fuck knew. Who the fuck cared. The woman was a genius. If you stayed on Einstein's good side. Get on her bad side—say by eating the last apple specially imported from the colonies—and you might get locked in your room with the computer refusing to answer and the food replicator spitting out a foul-smelling mush.

"Remember, no communication once on board. Stick to the plan." One last muttered instruction.

"Aye, aye, Captain."

"Don't fuck this up," Jameson growled.

"Who, me?"

"Let's not forget what happened in the Ashiesha system."

The captain would remind him of their banishment from there. As if it was Damon's fault the wife of the emperor seduced him. She'd pretended to be a servant. He'd thought her dazzled by his looks. The emperor was overcome with jealous anger. Damon's balls still tucked tight when they remembered how close he came to being emasculated.

"If you ask me, the Ashiesha thing was a blessing. They were cheap bastards, always trying to stiff us on the fees."

"Hmmph." Jameson took on a stony countenance as they approached the airlock after what seemed like an Earthen mile. Ships couldn't dock too closely together. The galactic winds and tides could sometimes cause them to collide. It was why the tunnels had flexibility to them.

The door to the other ship slid open at their approach, the matte black surface not reflecting anything. The Kanishqui possessed sleek ships, the exterior of them coated in some kind of shit—real excrement he might add—that provided a tough outer shell and protected the more fragile components from bits of galactic debris that could punch even through thick rock. It was why most crews used machines rather than suits for repairs when in deep space. One little piece of dust could kill.

Immediately upon stepping on the other ship, the moist air hit Damon's face, a wet towel slapping him with instant humidity. Within his uniform—black on black tunic over shirt tucked into pants—he thanked the fabric that wicked the sweat from his body and kept him cool. It did nothing for his lungs. At least he didn't choke or drown. The air might prove thick and cloying, but it was breathable.

Many of the species in space required an oxygen-based atmosphere. Those that didn't? Usually at war with those that did. Eradicating intolerance on Earth didn't mean humanity managed the same in space.

But a wary truce did exist between the wars spanning galaxies, and currently most of humanity was on peaceful terms with the Kanishqui. Although that could change shortly.

Entering the other ship meant being at the mercy of the Kanishqui. Good thing Damon boasted balls of tungsten. He managed a slightly bored expression and kept his hand off the holster of his gun. A gun he might not be allowed to keep, currently set to stun.

No killing. I promised.

Harder than it sounded, especially when they were met by the commander and a pair of guards. Knowing they were outnumbered—especially when it came to arms versus tentacles—his first instinct was to draw his weapon. The captain had insisted only the two of them meet with the Kanishqui commander. This was supposed to be a friendly, catching-up visit.

It would probably end with someone getting hurt. *By me.*

As the captains exchanged pleasantries, Damon peeked around. The interior of the Kanishqui ship held an ornate lavishness not seen on the *Gypsy Moth*—named after the rare insect Jameson had located in the clouds of Veynuz Nine and sold for a fortune. The Kanishqui vessel had a long title of *The Bucket That Carries the Liquid Vomited Remains*. The Kanishqui weren't known for their elegant prose.

But they could build nice ships. The exterior was slick and smooth, unlike their own vessel with its patched hull and thick seams.

The interior walls of the alien ship were gilded in a copper-colored metal that absorbed shadows. Strange property, and something that had Damon checking to see if his shadow returned every time he got away from the stuff.

The floor, a gray-green color, possessed a slimy surface that gripped the soles of his boots and removed the need for a gravity generator. The Kanishqui didn't actually walk. They preferred to float in order to avoid having their tentacles rubbed raw—which an enthusiastic human inventor once tried to solve. He apparently approached the race with an idea of creating shoes for the appendages. Even shoved some sample versions onto some tentacles. It didn't go well.

The Kanishqui were a proud bunch who brought new meaning to the term ugly. Really fucking ugly. They reminded Damon of the ancient pictures of octopi on Earth. Giant, bulbous head/body and arms. Lots of them. Unlike their Earth counterparts, though, the Kanishqui had evolved enough to not only emerge from the oceans and form a space-faring society, but also to manipulate their biology enough they could mate with just about any race in the galaxy—so long as it was a water-based biology, like humans. It made for some freaky-looking kids.

The alien speech held a particularly interesting gargle to it. As if they spoke through a mouthful of water. It could be as melodic as a babbling brook or as harsh as the slap of a wave on a rock.

But Damon understood each ripple of liquid, each rolling wave. The translator embedded into his auditory channels—which was a polite way of saying jammed into his ear and fused to the drum—communicated directly with his brain so that he heard the actual speech. What his translator couldn't do was make it interesting.

He tuned in to find his captain and the ugly Kanishqui leader yapping about the usual boring stuff.

"Looking mighty fit," Jameson remarked. "Have you been working out?"

Gargle, spit, swallow. *Lifting some weights. Eating my enemies.*

Funny how many species considered the ingestion

of sentient races as a necessary thing for strength. Some still believed they absorbed the knowledge and power of the entity they ate. In the case of the K'ahmelons—a bipedal winged reptile race from the jungle planets in the Rinfrst Galaxy—they truly did.

"I hear your last battle netted you a case of ice wine from the Ekiimo plains." Jameson arched a brow and lifted a plain box with no markings on it, yet the giant green Kanishqui quivered in excitement. "I brought chocolate."

More valuable than gold, chocolate was a hot commodity in the galaxy. As was coconut in any form, maple syrup, and corn. It turned out Earth had been on the right course when they played with ethanol as a fuel source. It made Earth a rich planet once they got the refinery of it right—with a little alien help.

Having all this natural wealth in one spot made Earth a target. Good thing they could afford the security to protect it. Nowadays, getting back to visit the first planet—because humans had long colonized dozens of others—proved almost impossible unless you had connections. It was a place that was split between manufacturing and a playground for the rich. Even the government didn't have a place on that coveted world. The Earth's government—known as the Gaia Federation—ruled from a massive space station built at the edge of the galaxy.

Each species had its own government. Some species that had spread to multiple galaxies often had more than one government. The universe was a mishmash of creatures, which meant a lot of treaties. Those that didn't want to play nicely with others went to war.

Other wars were fought over resources because, while there were lots of planets in the many solar systems, some of them lacked goods to trade—or had stripped their planets clean. Those that didn't have, conquered or sold their services to help others conquer. For example, the purple mercenaries, known as the Kulin, from Aressotle, made great for-hire soldiers. And they didn't require much pay if allowed to salvage the remains of Earth's enemies.

They didn't used to work as allies. In centuries past, the Kulin used to kidnap human women to make babies for them. They weren't the only ones stealing bodies. Back in the twenty-first century, there was a rash of alien abductions. It and other incursions by aliens was what eventually led to their discovery and humans finally being allowed to join the ranks of galactic travelers and players.

Three hundred EC years later and humans had multiplied and spread. Some likened them to an invasive weed that, once taken from its habitat with proper controls, multiplied.

With that many humans, each with different points of view, came division. Rival groups. Unlike the Kanishqui who were a tight-knit family group whose massive ships housed generations. Kind of like what the Rhomanii—the space gypsies—did on a smaller scale.

Remember, these are our allies. Didn't make his trigger finger any less itchy.

Damon followed the commanders a few paces back with one of the guards. The other one glided ahead.

He tuned in to listen as he fought the suction of the floor with each step.

Waves lapping. Gentle drip. *I have a daughter coming of age.*

Talk about jumping right into it.

Jameson shook his head. "Kind of you to offer, but I'll have to pass. My current relationship status is complicated."

Just a bit. Married to a woman who'd disappeared several EC years ago. For some reason, the captain wouldn't apply to have their union dissolved. Said he couldn't. Which was weird. And none of Damon's business.

But he had to wonder what the daughter looked like. He'd met the ugly Kanishqui leader—whose name sounded like "tinkle-tinkle-splash" and translated to "Flows-In-Spurts-From-Spout," nicknamed Fizz—before when he and the captain had done business. This was the first time a more permanent alliance was offered.

Fizz floated along the wide corridor, his tentacles suctioning to bits of walls. He pulled himself along, letting the lack of gravity float his bulky body. On their home world, where they had to deal with gravity, they'd constructed cities of flowing water. Their roads wide canals. Their highways raging rivers. A beautiful place, actually. If you weren't afraid of drowning.

They arrived at a grand set of doors, ornate and meant to impress. They slid open and displayed Fizz's lush personal quarters. Despite his rank as first mate, Damon and the guards weren't invited in; however, his captain did turn to say, "I'll buzz you when the fine commander and I are done."

In other words, piss off.

Damon waited until the doors shut before saying, "What do you say we go find ourselves some geer?" The galactic version of beer. Sometimes made with fuel.

One of the guards replied, a toilet swirling.

Damon made a face. "Wow, that was totally uncalled for. I mean, if you can't handle the fact a human can outdrink you, then just say so. No need to insult my man parts." He knew better than to compare his manhood with that of the Kanishqui. Damned thing was long and agile enough to do things even human women craved. The babies were butt ugly, though. "Just thought since the captain won't need me for a bit, we'd go hang and toss a few back."

Spit tossed and caught. Gurgle.

"Still on duty, eh? I totally get it. Of course, you need to work because your commander is obviously too big of a sushi to take care of himself against my wee captain. Because look at us, we're so scary." Damon lifted his hands and rolled his eyes.

If there was one thing that was common from one

species to another, it was pride. Prick it and you could manipulate it to get anything.

In this case, his new pal, Phlegmy-Water-Hitting-Mud, brought him down a few levels, via stairs of all things, to a massive cafeteria.

There were numerous liquid tanks embedded in the floor, the surface of each a different hue depending on the plankton it was seeded with. Within a few vats floated other things, lively aquatic things that required chewing. Massive canisters lined the walls, full of replenishing fluids. The Kanishqui didn't believe in replicated food. It meant they shopped for ingredients often. Unfortunately for the worlds they shopped from, they didn't always pay market value. And they sometimes took the inhabitants for a snack.

The cafeteria wasn't their final destination. Good thing, because Damon didn't see anything he wanted to put in his mouth. Not even the pink tentacle of the female who blew wet bubbles at him, lounging in the orange vat.

His buddy, whom he nicknamed Flem, skedaddled past, never glancing back to see if his human companion followed. Why bother when his trailing tentacles, equipped with auditory receptors, peeked for him.

Within the cafeteria, the floor didn't have as much tackiness, all the slopping liquid from the vats ruining its sticky trait. However, a good leap could cover a lot of ground so long as he was careful not to land in a vat.

Damon wasn't the only one hopping on two legs,

which was probably why most of the dining Kanishqui didn't pay him any mind. Damon noted the humans in gray overalls keeping the deck clean, squeegeeing the extra moisture into grates for recycling. Others guided large buckets on wheels to stock the vats. A few of the humans had ditched their coveralls and were being diddled in corners. Willingly, he might add.

Exiting the cafeteria, they immediately entered a kitchen-type prep area packed with even more humans. Not slaves, he noted. They were too happy and talkative for that. Instead of the staff uniform, a good many wore bright layers of fabric as they sat perched peeling and prepping. Food for the servants. A sign of a good ship. The starships that offered a place to live, protection, and regular meals tended to have no issues finding people to staff their vessels. The galaxy wasn't an easy place for those without work or credits to their names.

Damon counted himself lucky Jameson had snared him as a boy before he got into too much trouble. The captain set him on an entirely new life course. Mind you, he still got in trouble, but he considered that part of his charm. Damon figured he couldn't be all bad, considering he enjoyed a large circle of friends.

Pity he couldn't have brought a friend or two with him. The deeper he went into the ship, the more he was conscious of how far he had to travel to return to the *Moth*. The good news was, in this place, he no longer felt alone and cut off from his kind. Did Flem even realize just how screwed he was if the humans on board decided to revolt? Because they sure as hell outnumbered those who owned the ship.

Another level down, and they finally reached the bowels of the ship, the hidden heart where the things the crew didn't want the commander of the ship to see happened.

They had a hidden heart on the *Gypsy Moth,* too. Captain Jameson knew about it, of course, but allowed it so long as the crew didn't cross any hard lines.

In the hideaway zone, fraternizing occurred, usually helped along by some drinking. The alcoholic kind.

In space, both drinking and kissing of coworkers was frowned upon. Everyone worked closely together on a ship, which meant extra care was needed to ensure harmony amongst everyone. No one wanted to be the one left behind at a galactic way station because there was friction on board.

However, denial bred a need to flout the rules. To feel free. Humans needed a chance to unwind. Flirt. Have fun and forget they were hurtling through space and putting a lot of faith in mechanics and engineering.

Music pulsed from speakers strung on the ceiling. It alternated from a water orchestra to a hard-pulsing beat. In the hidden heart, humans and Kanishqui mingled. A quick glance showed probably about two dozen bodies milling around. Some dressed in dull gray uniforms, others in civilian clothes. Everyone present looking for a good time.

It wasn't hard to find the bar serving drinks and to

snare a glass. The bartender, a flinty-eyed guy with a shaven head and a goodly number of piercings, held out his hand for payment. Good thing Damon had brought a hunk of chocolate. Never leave the ship without it.

Damon used the sweet treat to buy Flem a drink as well. "A toast," Damon declared, holding up his glass. "To space." He tossed back the drink then signaled for another round.

Once the glasses hit the bar—and stuck to the tacky surface—he dug into his pocket and withdrew a stoppered tube. He shook it. "Interest you in a sprinkle of cocoa?" he asked.

The drool coming from Flem was a strong yes. Damon shook a bit of the chocolate powder into the glass. Flem downed it and slapped the glass back down, and not a moment too soon. A jiggle went through him and all his tentacles wiggled.

"Good shit, eh?" Damon remarked. Chocolate was valuable because many species reacted to it like a drug. Humans, the universe's biggest drug dealers. "More?"

The frantic flail said yes.

They drew some attention. The Kanishqui crowded around.

"Don't worry, boys and girl," he said with a wink at a mauve female. "I've got plenty." He tilted the cocoa over numerous glasses at once and pulled out more vials as more glasses hit the bar. Much drinking occurred. Damon kept up with his hosts and showed off by tossing back two shots, one after another. Fucking rocket fuel burning down his throat.

He slammed down the glasses and declared, "Double fisted."

Waterfall crashing. *challenge accepted. Nine tentacles slapped down on the table. An empty glass rolled from each, not a hint of chocolate left behind.

"Refill." He tipped in more powder.

Not that Flem needed more. His many-armed new friend was singing, and not very well. Rapids crashing on rocks then babbling softly. Not that Flem cared how it sounded. He and his other tentacled friends were swaying along in time, weeds in a current. Which was Damon's cue.

"I gotta take a leak," Damon announced, getting to his feet.

"I wondered when you'd break the seal." A buxom woman, gray hair scraped back into a bun, winked. "Come with me. I'll take ye to the lavatory." The matron with the wide hips led the way out of the party atmosphere of the hidden heart into a service corridor.

Damon wasted no time. He located the handle to a chute, dragged it open, and whipped out his dick for a piss. While the medical injection he'd taken ensured he couldn't get drunk, it did nothing to empty his bladder. The relief made him groan.

His contact kindly looked away while he did his business, but she did laugh. "Was it as good for you as for me?"

"Better," he said with a grin. "I'm Damon." He

tucked everything away and placed his hands under the bacterial cleanser before turning to offer it for a shake.

"Matilda."

"Ever notice, Matilda, how moths come at night?"

"Only if there's light."

He smiled. He'd found his contact. "Where to?"

"First..." Matilda held out her hand.

He reached into his breast pocket and withdrew a small amulet. Favors always came with a cost. He wasn't sure what made the amulet valuable. The captain had given it to him along with the code phrase and mission. Whatever it was, it satisfied his contact.

Pocketing it, she said, "Follow me."

Good thing she was there to guide him because no way could Damon have found his way, even with a map. The route they took proved circuitous, and yet they met no one but humans on their way. The utility areas were considered below a Kanishqui. No interference or awkward questions meant Damon might actually accomplish his mission without getting into trouble.

Might being highly unlikely.

"How much farther?" he asked.

Matilda glanced at him over her shoulder. "We are close now. It's taking longer because the route we took is surveillance free."

"Speaking of surveillance, did you need extraction for doing this?" Damon asked as they climbed yet another ladder.

"I'll be fine. The blame for what happens next will be placed on your drinking companion. He was assigned to keep watch on you."

Poor Flem. Another chocoholic... Damon wondered what rehab was like.

Matilda placed a finger by her lips before turning the next corner. She crept, and when she paused, she dropped to her haunches.

With another gesture for quiet, the matron peered out through a grill.

"It's clear. Let's go. She's in the last cell at the end."

She, as in his target. The whole reason for being on this ship, for "accidentally" running into the Kanishqui in the first place.

The grill popped out, and Matilda gestured him forth.

"Aren't you coming?" he asked when he noticed Matilda still behind the grill.

"This is as far as I go."

"How the hell do I get back out?" Because the place was a maze.

"The deal was to show you the way."

"I can't go back the same way with the cargo."

"It will cost you." Matilda held out her hand. He dropped the last of his pure chocolate in it. She quickly told him how to exit, no guiding him this time. Now he just had to remember it.

The door at the end of the hall bore an actual metal hasp. No electronic locks. No wasting of ship power on that.

"Stand back from the door," he ordered.

No reply. He'd have to assume she heard him. He placed his weapon on low and aimed it at the lock, melting it. Yanking the door open, he stepped in and was clobbered.

CHAPTER 2

"Oww! Do you mind?" the stranger snapped. "I'm here to rescue you."

Michonne—Michi for short—stared at the man rubbing his chest. "Who are you?" Other than ridiculously handsome with dark hair and blue eyes.

"Your fucking knight in shining armor."

The profanity had her wrinkling her nose. "Is that language necessary?"

"Fucking right it is." He pointed to his ribs. "You're not the one who's going to have a bruise."

She chewed on her lower lip. She had hit him rather hard. The stool they'd given her to sit on made a lovely weapon. One she aimed too low. The man in her cell was much too tall.

Clasping her hands, she rocked on her tiptoes. "Did my father send you?"

"What do you think? I am not doing this out of the kindness of my heart, sweetheart."

A term of endearment already? But they'd just met! How forward of him. And intriguing. Father usually kept her away from the rakish sorts.

"Let me gather my things."

"Things? Why would you bring any of their stuff with you?" The handsome man frowned.

Did he not understand how things worked? "These are my things. I've been prepared for my abduction for a long while now." A bag packed with her necessities so that, when it finally happened, she was ready. She'd learned enough from her sisters to know what to expect. Why, Linnette had been kidnapped before she'd reached twenty EC years. She now had a brood of seven children, three palaces, and a vacation moon to herself. So lucky.

Michi, on the other hand, had been taken by a Kanishqui. Not exactly her ideal. But this new fellow... While he didn't have sleek, blue skin like her sister's husband, he was handsome. Even if he scowled.

"We need to move, princess."

"Rushing leads to mistakes." She remembered the lessons from her governess and shared her knowledge to make the universe a better place.

"Stalling can kill. Let's go." He snared her pink satchel. What a gentleman to carry her things. What she didn't appreciate as much was his grabbing of her hand.

She pulled it free, or at least attempted to. "Unhand me. This is most unseemly."

"I don't have time for manners. We need to move."

He yanked her, and she stumbled before catching her feet.

"Must you drag me?" she gasped as she practically ran down the hall to keep pace. She gripped her skirts in one hand to keep them from tangling in her legs.

"Do you always question your rescuers this much?" he replied. He stopped at the intersection, just before the corner. He eased around to peek on both sides then pulled her left.

"I expected a rescue with a touch more chivalry."

"I'll take survival over politeness, princess. If you don't mind."

She could see how that might be a better plan.

He stopped abruptly, and she ran into his back. His very broad back.

For a moment, he didn't move, and she said, "I am glad you made an appearance when you did. The choices given to me by the commander were rather limited. Marriage or dinner." Neither appealed.

"Fizz wants to marry you?"

"No need to sound so surprised. I'm considered quite the catch." No need for modesty when the truth sufficed.

"Why did you say no? I hear they can make excellent lovers." He shot her a look over his shoulder and a wink.

Her cheeks heated. "I am not looking for a lover. And if I were, it wouldn't be with a Kanishqui." Saying it aloud seemed so blasphemous. But Michi couldn't help it. She wanted to at least marry someone who had only two arms and two legs. She could handle even two heads, but one penis was preferred. Although her freak of a sister, Priscilla, enjoyed otherwise.

"You won't have to sleep with anyone if you can follow instructions long enough for us to get off this ship. Don't listen to me and maybe you will find out how you feel about having sex with sushi."

"Sushi?" she said questioningly.

"Raw fish you put in your mouth."

"That's disgusting!" she exclaimed. If grossly entertaining.

"Actually, in some places, eating sushi is a delicacy. For the Kanishqui, it's known as foreplay. I hear they're kind of rubbery, though."

Her lips quirked. "Shouldn't we be escaping rather than discussing the cannibalism of my captors?"

"We are escaping. Which reminds me, according to Matilda, the next part is gonna be tricky. We're going to enter the hall where the docking tunnels are. It will probably be guarded."

"Guarded. I see. You need help fighting them given your skill level is subpar." She caught his dilemma right away.

He frowned. "My skills are fine. I can handle a few of the Kanishquis."

Could he? She eyed his two arms.

"I'm stronger than you think," he blustered.

"If you can fight them, then I don't see the problem."

"Captain left orders to not kill them."

"Then knock them out."

The man turned to look over his shoulder. As if he could see past the bend. "Knock them out, she says. They're liking hitting gelatine."

"Doesn't your weapon have a stun setting?"

"Yeah, but using it, even on stun, will likely set off an alarm."

"Are you trying to tell me you can't get us out of here?" She fluttered her lashes at him. "Oh dear. How disappointing. We might as well return to my cell."

"You're not going back."

"And according to you, we can't go forward because you can't fight." An odd choice for a rescuer.

His face tightened. His lips flattened. Then he sighed. "We're getting out of here."

"What of the guards?"

"I'll handle them. Let's go."

Stepping around the bend, she heard the liquid words of her captors, but only barely over the racing of her heart. This was all so very frightening—and exciting.

Michi had led a very sheltered life to this point. Closely guarded by her father, a treasure for the stealing because of her worth. Unlike her older sisters, Michi had reached a ripe old age of twenty-three EC years and still remained unfettered. Not for lack of trying. Many attempts to abduct had been made. An alliance with Papa was worth the trouble. But up until now, those attempts were foiled.

Which was why the success of the Kanishqui

shocked. Of all the potential captors, couldn't she have gotten a handsome one? Someone like the man still holding her hand? He had a callused grip, unlike that of her tutors. Scholars tended to have soft skin. Father had tough hands. He didn't start out rich and powerful. He worked hard to get where he was. They learned his story early in the schoolroom.

As predicted, a pair of floating Kanishquis guarded a door. The one closest to them gargled something.

"Who's the girl?" Her rescuer didn't even look back at her. "I picked her up on the lower level. Cute, ain't she? We were going to visit my crib for some action, if you know what I mean."

Warble. Swirl.

"Share?" He tossed an amused grin back at her. "No, I don't think she's into that kind of thing. But I could be wrong. Let me ask."

"No." Heat flooded her skin once again. The very idea.

"You heard the lady, so if you'll kindly move to the side."

The Kanishqui guards held their ground. Or, given they floated, was the correct term air?

"Really, guys, you gonna cock block a man who's been in space for way too long?" That was the only warning they got before the gun sitting in his holster ended up aimed at the guards.

He fired. Bright yellow flashes that stunned the Kanishqui—but didn't kill. They floated in the air, tentacles adrift.

"You left them alive." Definitely not a true mercenary.

"Duh. I promised the captain." He tucked away the gun and held out his hand. "Come on. Ship's just over there." Over there being through a flexible tunnel that hadn't seen the factory of its birth for a long time.

"That doesn't look safe."

"Safer than staying here. Let's go."

She took a step, and a tentacle wrapped around her ankle. She wobbled and yelped.

He pulled his gun and fired again. The tentacle went limp, but the other guard, also still awake, managed to sound an alarm.

Her rescuer shot him again, too, but not before a klaxon roared to life. The door to the connecting tube slammed shut. The entire section they stood in sealed itself off with a clang.

Her rescuer groaned. "Fuck me. They've trapped us."

"What does this mean?" she asked. Because, if he was perturbed, it probably didn't bode well.

"It means either the commander of this vessel has to declare an all clear to unlock the doors or we need the *Gypsy Moth* to punch a hole in the hull, without killing us, that we can use to escape."

"But we have no space suits."

"Yeah, we might get some space bite. Maybe lose a few extremities, depending on how long we're exposed."

"Is there a third choice?" Because the first was

improbable and the second most definitely hazardous to their health—and limbs.

"No other choices, princess. And given number two is the Hail Mary of space, we need to work on the first option. Find a way to convince the commander to let us go." He paced, avoiding the floating tentacles of the unconscious guards.

"You're a visitor to his ship. Perhaps you could demand safe passage."

"I won't be able to demand a pot to piss in once Fizz sees you."

"Who is Fizz?"

"The commander. And he's gonna have a hissy fit when he sees I'm stealing you."

"It's not stealing but rescuing because I am a person, not a thing," she announced, straightening to her full height, which didn't quite make his chin.

"If you were a thing, I wouldn't have listened to you and I'd have found a way to draw off the guards rather than shoot them."

Her eyes widened. "You're blaming me for your ineptitude in planning my rescue? Perhaps, were you better equipped or trained, we wouldn't be in this dilemma."

His jaw dropped as he recognized the obvious weakness of his attempt thus far.

"Are you for fucking real?" he said, trying to shock with his profanity.

"Very real." She'd come out of the womb perfect. "I will admit to being surprised by your lack of skills.

Father usually hires more competent people." Her sister Navinda got saved from her marriage to an Ymp—who were notorious womanizers—before he'd even had a chance to expose himself to her in the getaway ship. She then turned around to marry her mercenary, who turned out to be a notorious pirate king.

Michi's rescuer didn't wear an eye patch or look half as dangerous as Navinda's husband. But he was much handsomer, if annoying.

"Maybe your father doesn't like you as much as his other daughters," he muttered.

She blinked. "Are you implying my father dislikes me and is intentionally botching my rescue?"

"Are you calling me shitty at my job?" He raised a brow in her direction.

She clamped her lips tight.

"That's what I thought." He turned around to look at the door to the docking tube. "The alarm's already going. Guess it won't matter if I use this." He fiddled with his pistol before he raised it.

While not an engineer, she saw a problem with his plan. "Won't that compromise the seal?"

"Probably. Got a better plan?"

Surely there was a way out of this situation that didn't involve dying from a hull breach or marrying the Kanishqui commander.

The siren went silent, which seemed more ominous than the wailing.

"We are out of time, princess." He steadied his

weapon, and she threw herself on his arm before he could fire it.

"Wait. I have an idea." One brewing since the moment she saw him.

"Does it have a working transporter in it? Because ours is on the fritz."

She shook her head, the heavy loops of her braided hair threatening to spill. "If it works, then the Kanishqui will let us go."

"Just like that?" He didn't attempt to hide a skeptical note. "I highly doubt that."

"It will work. Trust me."

"The last woman who said that took out lube and a ridged vegetable. Didn't work for her, won't work for you."

"I'm not making a salad."

"And we're out of time." A hum farther down the hall indicated the door had opened. He squinted at the portal. "When you hear the hiss, grab hold of me. Once the door pops open, we'll have to run through the tube and hope we make it to the other side."

"I told you, we don't have to fight. What's your name?"

"I don't see—"

She cut him off. "Name."

"First mate, Damon Faulkner."

Not a captain. Pity. But he'd have to do. "Lovely to meet you, Damon Faulkner. Now, please repeat after me. I indubitably, without a doubt, say I do."

"What?"

"Say it. I indubitably, without a doubt, say I do."

"I indubitably, without a doubt, say I do?"

Said as a query and yet that was all she needed. The code phrase to make it work. Michi pressed her lips to Damon's, an impromptu kiss that caught him off guard.

Caught her off guard, too, because it jolted her with an electric zing that tickled her all the way to her toes, and especially between the thighs.

He sucked in a breath. Opened his mouth. Deepened the kiss. Set her senses aflame. But she couldn't forget why she embraced him. She grabbed hold of his bottom lip with her teeth, a firm grip, then bit down. Hard enough to break skin. She needed blood to activate it.

Damon yelled and pulled away. "What the fuck, princess?" He wiped his hand over his lip, taking with it the bead of blood.

Too late to erase what she'd done. She ran her tongue along the smooth enamel of her tooth, the insignia that used to sit there gone. Just in time. The tentacles of her former fiancé appeared before his bulbous body.

She stood beside her rescuer, hands folded primly in front of her.

A human accompanied the Kanishqui commander, a man in a black uniform much like her rescuer. The pants a supple leather tucked into high matte polished boots. The shirt, a silky fabric, billowy all over, tapered at the waist and wide at the shoulders.

Spit. Spray. Jiggle. *What's going on here? How dare you attack my people.*

Damon held out his hands in a conciliatory gesture. "I understand this might seem a little unorthodox. But I can explain—"

This was her cue. Michi stepped in front of him and interrupted. "There you are. About time you appeared so I could make my excuses."

You aren't going anywhere.

"Yes I am. Remember how I told you we couldn't marry?" She turned sideways and pointed to her rescuer. "This is why. Meet my husband."

"Husband?" Damon squeaked. Which made her wonder what kind of modifications he'd undergone. She'd emerged perfect from the womb, her genetic sequence fine-tuned ahead of time to ensure she was everything her parents wanted. A perfect daughter. A tool for making alliances and enriching the family. Father might take issue with her choice in husband, given Damon was not only common but not even the highest-ranking person on board his ship.

Gurgle, splash? Fizz quivered with question.

She rolled a shoulder. "Yes, I know he's a border-line pirate." She whirled and gazed at Damon. "But who cares about that? He's got the dreamiest eyes. And the nicest voice. And... *Sigh*..." The gushing was for the Kanishqui's benefit. Would Damon have the wits to grasp the drama she enacted?

For a second, he stared dumbly then caught on. "When I heard my darling spouse was taken, I thought it must be a mistake. I mean, who steals another man's wife?"

"Which is why," the captain said, taking over, "we didn't mention it when we contacted you. Especially since I'm sure your taking of my first mate's spouse was completely accidental on your part."

Water over pebbles.

"No, we haven't been married long," Damon replied. "Still practically honeymooners, which is why I acted rashly." Reaching out, he grasped her around the waist and lifted her, just the right height for the kiss he planted on her lips.

He's kissing me. And without permission, but she couldn't exactly protest—*he is my husband.* Nor did she want to since it proved as electric as before. For her at least. She could have kissed him all day. He, though, wanted to talk. "Quick thinking," he murmured quietly amidst moans. Hers, she should add.

"Mmmm."

He set her down—pity—and tucked her behind him. "Captain, now that I've found my wife, I demand satisfaction. The commander of this vessel unlawfully stole my woman."

"The evidence is pretty damning. Care to explain?" The captain didn't bat an eye as he queried the giant blob.

She wasn't married when I took her.

"Even if I wasn't, I wouldn't marry you." She lifted her chin.

A warm urine stream on a piling mound of...

Her mouth rounded. "Oh, that was foul."

"Take that insult back." Damon stood tall and offended. "You can't talk about my wife like that."

Warm squirt on a favorite blanket.

Damon huffed. "You hear how he insults me, Captain?"

"My man is right. You are insulting us all." The captain held up a hand as the Kanishqui gurgled a stream. "Nope. You can forget that case of chocolate I was going to give you. And definitely no alliance with your family. Really. I thought better of you than stealing a man's wife."

Drip. Drip.

"I do understand their marriage wasn't common knowledge, but you are aware of it now and still refuse to let my man leave with his wife. Unacceptable. You can consider our trading deal off."

Gurgle, siphon?

"Talk? We will only talk once you let me and my man off this ship."

Water down a drain. *You may leave as a measure of my respect for the captain.*

The door to the docking tube suddenly opened, yet Damon did not smile or relax. He laced his fingers through Michi's. "Shall we, *wife?*"

She held her head high as she entered the tube. This wasn't one of the more elegant ones with a moving walkway and music. It was opaque, yet blurry, giving the outside silhouettes of the ships a sinister shape. The stars were fuzzy distant balls. She gripped Damon's hand tight, willing him to go faster.

They might have fast-talked the Kanishqui into letting them go, but it would be best if they got out of there in case they changed their minds.

Only once they exited the tube and the door to the ship sealed shut behind them did her rescuer laugh.

"Damn, princess, that was the perfect ploy to get him to release us."

She pursed her lips. Now for the possibly unpleasant part. "It wasn't a ploy. We are married."

He snickered. "Sure, we are."

"We are married. Have been since that first kiss."

"Hate to break it to you, my naïve princess, but it takes more than a smooch to make it so."

"I know it takes more than a kiss, which is why you also have to repeat the trigger phrase."

He stopped laughing. "Hold on, are you serious?"

A bob of her head and she explained. "I knew that I had to make it real in case the Kanishqui commander demanded proof. Which is why you wear my mark."

"Mark?" he repeated slowly while his captain, who had more manners and would have probably made a better rescuer, ignored them to bark out orders to his crew to get them moving, sooner rather than later.

"Yes, mark. On the inside of your lip." She tapped her bottom one. "You'll find my crest tattooed on your flesh. It identifies you as my lawful husband."

"You marked me?" He again squeaked, bringing into question his gene quality.

"It is how we marry in my religion." Dkar—a relatively young religion—was only two centuries old and discovered by humans during their explorations, adopted and adapted and gaining ground among the wealthy.

"But I never agreed to marry you," Damon sputtered.

"You said the ritual words."

"I didn't know what I was saying. I certainly never meant it."

"Nonetheless"—she shrugged—"it's binding."

Although she really wished it weren't when he uttered, "I don't fucking believe this," and left.

It was an intriguing change of pace from the males who'd been trying to maneuver her into choosing them for years. Males who either tried to woo her into marking them or, like the Kanishqui, coerced her into doing it.

Doesn't this Damon Faulkner realize the honor I paid him by choosing him?

Apparently not, since he left her to fend for herself on a strange ship.

She glared at the door he'd left through while the captain cleared his throat.

"Despite knowing your father, I don't think we've ever met. I'm Captain Jameson of the *Gypsy Moth*."

Casting a glance at him, she spent a brief moment admiring his dark skin, his vivid green eyes, and engaging smile.

"I meet very few of my father's allies and friends."

He kept his daughters sequestered lest the wrong person be tempted. "Why is it you sent your first mate to save me rather than do it yourself?" He would have been a perfect choice for a husband.

"I couldn't." The captain turned over his arm and raised his sleeve, displaying a tattoo.

Already taken. Figured.

"Thank you for providing assistance." She remembered her manners.

"I have to admit I was surprised when your father contacted me. It's been awhile since we did business."

"Father never forgets who his allies are."

"You are unharmed?"

"Physically, yes." But her irritation was rather elevated given her abandonment by her husband.

"And you truly did marry Damon?"

"As per the ways of the Dkar. Your first mate doesn't seem pleased."

"You took him by surprise." The gravelly tone didn't match his smooth looks.

"He'd better get used to it." Because the marriage, while unplanned, was binding. For him at least.

He'd better stop aggravating me, or this wouldn't go well for him.

CHAPTER 3

Married? Surely the princess lied.

Damon ran to the nearest communal washroom area. The wall held a mirror over the trough sink. He leaned forward and checked his lip where she'd bitten him. Saw just the tender remains of the cut. It had already begun to heal because of the vitamins he took to boost his system.

No mark to be seen.

She lied. He was fine no matter what she said. He used the washroom, ridding himself of the last of the booze, and was washing his hands when Jameson appeared behind him.

"There you are. Hiding, are we?"

"Try pissing. Took more than a few shots to accomplish the mission. Those octopi bastards can drink like fish."

"At least the plan worked."

"As if there was any doubt we'd save the woman."

"Speaking of saving. You seem awfully calm considering what happened."

"You mean her claim we got married?" Damon scoffed. "Just fucking with me apparently. There's no mark. See?" He jutted his lower lip.

Jameson shook his head. "It's not going to show on the outside of your lip. Look inside your mouth."

"I'm not looking because there's nothing there. I know how the mating marks work." Rings welded to fingers. Tattoos that couldn't be covered by makeup on the body. The Jemmyni actually fused their bodies together. He shoved up his sleeves and held out his hands, flipping them over. "Nothing. She didn't have enough time to do any of that."

"Did she bite you?"

"Yeah." No point in denying it.

"Then she marked you. Look inside your lip."

Damon wanted to stubbornly say no. He couldn't be married. He'd not agreed. He wasn't ready for that, and especially not with a prim and a little-too-proper princess—with a bossy side.

However, he wanted to know. He leaned forward again and pulled his lip forward. Almost celebrated until he noticed it low down inside, a silvery emblem tattooed inside his mouth. "Wha da fuk?" he said, lip still extended. He whirled. "Sha makked me." His words emerged slightly garbled.

The captain arched a brow. "Does this mean you'll be expecting a wedding present?"

Damon glared.

"And time off for a honeymoon?"

He intensified the glare.

"Don't look at me like that. I'm not the one who let some strange woman suck my mouth."

"She told me to trust her."

"Was this before or after you shot the guards?"

"She dared me."

It was the captain's turn to give him a look.

Damon rolled his shoulders. "Excuse me for being a guy for a minute."

"Trying being a first mate instead, would you?"

"Hey, she's safe, isn't she? As ordered. And I might add you could show a little more sympathy for my situation. You're not the one married." Only after he said it did he wince. No point in apologizing, the gaffe was made. They weren't supposed to mention the captain's missing wife.

"She's safe, but her father won't be pleased. She's his favorite, and she's married to you."

"So, we get divorced, no biggie."

Jameson scrubbed his hand over his face. "Actually, it's bigger than you understand."

"Because he's your friend. I totally get it. The situation is awkward. We'll just explain."

"Explaining won't do shit. The Dkar follow some fucked-up set of societal rules, their equivalent of a religion. One that doesn't believe in divorce."

"Whoa." Damon held up a hand. "No divorce?"

"Their marriages are binding from the moment the mark is transferred."

"That can't be right. We haven't even slept together."

"Doesn't matter."

"For how long?"

"Forever."

"What?" he yelped. "Seriously, how long?" Because amongst humans, marriages were contracts with set terms that included an expiry date.

"The Dkar are old school, so it's 'til death do you part."

Judging by the captain's face, he was serious. "Damn. That's crap. How healthy is she, do you figure?" He only knew the info he'd gotten going into the mission, which consisted of a picture and her first name, Michonne.

"She'll outlive you more than likely."

"Genes that good, huh?"

"Yes, but mostly because her father will likely kill you so they can reset the mark and have her ally with something he deems more worthy."

"Hold on, are you saying they're going to kill me so they can marry her off again?" Damon asked.

"Yes."

"That's a shit way to thank somebody for saving his daughter's life."

"If it's any consolation, I'll be thanked. Probably with a big transfer of credits and a case of something expensive."

"While I end up as space dust. Is it me, or is this

day getting worse and worse?" Damon groaned as he scrubbed his face with a hand.

Whoop. Whoop.

The ship sounded a warning alarm.

Jameson barked, "Rosy! Status report."

The ship's artificial intelligence—AI—recited a litany of reasons for the alarm. "The Kanishqui vessel has activated its shields. It is also arming its electro-cryogenic cannon."

Bad news. One blast from it and their ship would be dead in space for a few hours at least. Until the pulse wore off and the various systems—such as environmental and shields—came back online. Long enough, though, for them all to die.

The good thing about the damned cannon was it took time to charge. They had time to escape.

A better question was, why did the Kanishqui suddenly decide to attack?

Jameson marched out of the facilities, snapping orders aloud. "Keep sounding the alert. Have all active duty at their stations. Non-active on standby. Prep the engines for streaking."

"Shouldn't we be readying the shields?" Damon asked, keeping pace with his captain.

"Not this time. According to the latest engineering report, our second power cell is still offline, which means I want all the power going to the engines for departure. We're going to do a quick jump."

They entered the transport capsule—a rapid method of movement aboard the ship for those with the stomach for it. The captain only had to say, "Bridge," for it to zoom off.

"Why is the Kanishqui ship attacking us now? I thought everything was cool. Fizz let us go."

"And changed his mind."

"Is he stupid? We outgun him."

"We do. Yet he apparently thinks he can take us."

"So let's blast him out of the galaxy."

"We can't. And no, I don't care to explain why."

Knowing Jameson wouldn't do this without good reason, Damon gave a nod. "Whatever you say, sir. I'll head to engineering and ensure they're prepared for jump." Then it occurred to him. "What of your friend's daughter?" A beautiful woman, aggravating with her princess airs and even more annoying for her tricking him into marriage.

"Being shown to her quarters. I'll deal with your nuptials and her father once we've put some space between us and this quadrant."

The elevator capsule stopped and spat out the captain. Then it was Damon's turn to zip off into the bowels of the ship then farther still to the tail end of the ship where the engines were located behind the heaviest hulls.

Damon arrived in time for someone to yell, "Strap in. Going to streak, in five, four..." He dove against the wall and slid his arms through a harness a moment before the ship paused, as if hanging in anticipation, and then they were gone.

Streak, faster than sound and light. It had revolutionized space travel, especially since it proved a lot safer than wormhole travel. If you could plot the coordinates properly. Damon wouldn't pretend to understand the science behind it other than it did something that bent space and time and got a ship from point A to B without weeks or months of travel. But it could only be done in short bursts that required recharging in between. After fifteen minutes, the streak ended. During that time, Damon tapped into the ship via his embedded wrist com for a status report.

According to the logs, the *Moth* had moved before the Kanishqui managed to fire their cannon. A conflict averted until the next time they met. Then again, by the time they crossed paths again, things should have calmed themselves. And if not, the captain would invest in a few cases of chocolate as apology.

Exiting the harness—which existed all over the ship for the times they needed to streak with little notice, especially if they didn't want to end up flattened on a wall or tumbling down a corridor—Damon continued to the heart of engineering. He might as well have been on an alien planet. Or a magical realm. The bowels of the ship certainly had an ethereal appearance to them. The energy cores—contained within clear diamond cylinders that reached several stories—glowed, their color not on a spectrum he could describe. Their origin not earthly in nature—and expensive.

The captain had spent a fortune retrofitting his ship with the streak drive and upgraded power system.

Money well spent. Few could catch them when they streaked.

Taking the stairs two at a time down to the lower level, Damon nodded at some of the workers in this section. Most ignored him. Snobby bunch that kept to themselves. This wouldn't happen on a military vessel. The lack of respect might have bothered, except he knew they didn't do it on purpose.

The crew that worked in engineering weren't one hundred percent human anymore. The drives they worked in close proximity with had a tendency of changing biological matter after too much time spent in their proximity. This resulted in an engineering crew with, in some cases, more metal parts than human. Cyborgs, as they called themselves, had recently declared themselves their own species apart from humanity.

Not many argued about them splitting off. Anyone who encountered a cyborg noticed their difference— and he wasn't talking about their machine parts. They thought differently. Acted differently. He couldn't have said if it was the metal in their bodies or the alien technology they worked with that changed them, but the fact remained they were fucking weird.

Damon reached the main control area for the engine room—a circular hub, ringed in consoles with people bent over them, fingers flying. In their midst stood Craig "Crank" Abrams.

A massive man, over six feet and wide, his bald pate shone, his goatee was well trimmed and his uniform—with the sleeves torn off—showcased his metal arm from the shoulder down. He'd lost the limb trying to save his wife. Some claimed he'd also lost his heart when she died.

Crank didn't speak. He stood with arms crossed, and yet Damon knew he was directing everything that was going on. Yet another cyborg trait. Wireless communication. Handy, if eerie, at times like this when a man who had to use actual spoken words needed to interrupt.

"Crank, Captain sent me to check on the state of our engines." Which they already knew because of the reports, but given how engineering liked to recluse themselves, some kind of in-person checking was encouraged.

Crank didn't bother looking at him as he replied. "The status is still the same. We have one active power unit. As I've mentioned already, we need to stop and refuel the second one to see if the repairs worked."

"I do believe we're stopping in at the Xandu way station within the next few days."

"That will do. I will send you a revised list of items required."

"You know you could leave the ship and buy those things yourself on ship credit."

"I'm needed here."

More like he was hiding. And Damon couldn't help poking.

"You didn't show up at the last officer meeting."

Crank turned haunting clear blue eyes his way. "I was detained."

The man was always detained of late. "Still pissed, are you?" Crank hadn't yet forgiven Jameson for saving his life in the incident five years ago that took his wife.

"Emotion is a waste of time."

It sure was. And so was marriage. In the next few hours, as Damon checked in with the various stations on board, and after a few more streaks, he had had time to mull over the whole marriage thing.

What kind of working guy wanted to settle down with one person for life? Sure, some people liked it, but personally, Damon had yet to find a woman he could tolerate for a few days in a row let alone a lifetime. It was why he tended to curtail his onboard activities and waited for their visits to way stations and planets. A few days to a week refueling and enjoying rest and relaxation were easy to walk away from. Not to mention, departing for another galaxy made it hard for any sexual partners to cling or show up uninvited.

Marriage, though, when you worked aboard a ship, meant bringing your spouse with you. Sharing your space with someone else. Never being alone. Stuck with one vagina forever. It seemed worse in some respects than a prison sentence.

And to think he was stuck in a marriage. *I have a fucking wife.*

A cute wife.

But still? He was much too young to be tied down. He didn't care how wealthy she was. Damon wanted for nothing. He had his own spacious quarters, which, as first mate, were second only to the captain's.

He had enough credits in the Qpers Galactic Bank that he could buy all but the most extravagant items.

His genes, while not state-of-the-art, were modified enough to provide him good health, excellent recuperative abilities, long life, and good looks.

What else could a man ask for?

Marriage was a nightmare. Which was why he might have uttered a scream when he entered his quarters and found his wife sprawled across his bed and his room overtaken with clothes. Women's clothes. And a pink blanket. On his bed.

"What the fuck?"

CHAPTER 4

"About time you appeared." Michonne rolled on the bed to face her husband, who looked rather displeased. Probably tired after working all day. With her wealth, that would change. Soon he could be a man of leisure.

"What are you doing here?" He entered the room but didn't approach her. "Didn't someone show you to your quarters?"

"Yes."

"Then why are you here?"

"Because it's my room." She flipped back to her stomach and switched the interesting holoscreen of information she'd pulled up on her new husband to a meal menu instead.

"No, this is my room."

"Our room," she corrected. "We're married, remember?" She certainly couldn't forget the hotness of the kiss, the thrill as she finally marked a man as her own. Not the husband she'd expected, however she saw the raw possibility in him.

"About the whole marriage thing... Captain said it was binding."

"It is."

"Surely there's a way to annul it?"

"No. The seal is permanent. Only your death will remove it." It was to ensure no one could simply take the mark then murder her to inherit. The wealth only passed on through her—alive.

"We keep speaking of my death. What if you die?"

She cocked her head. "Thinking of killing me? That would be rude."

"No ruder than this discussion."

"Then to answer your question, if I die first, then you'll die soon after. The seal I placed on you links our lives together."

His lips flattened. "So, if you die, I die. If I die, you—"

"Marry again. I am the heiress, and until I have progeny of my own to cede my portion to, then I must survive at all costs to spread my family name."

"Don't you mean my name? You did, after all, marry me."

"No, I meant my name. In the Dkar religion, the higher-ranked person is the one whose last name is taken. It's how it works in my culture." To which only the wealthiest of families belonged. Invitation was by net worth or marriage only.

Her husband blinked. He had incredibly long, dark

lashes, the kind people paid to have. "I am not taking your last name, because we are not married."

"Denial won't change it." And his arguing really dropped him a few notches in her esteem. Perhaps the reports she'd perused were mistaken about his intelligence. Pity. Good thing she could have their children bio engineered to take after her.

"There must be a way to stop this. I don't want to be married." Poor man sounded so disgruntled, which was intriguing. Michi was used to males doing everything they could to get tied to her.

"Complaining won't change it."

"I'm not complaining. I'm lamenting the lack of choice in this affair. I mean, come on, even you have to admit I'm probably not what you envisioned as a husband."

She pretended to give it some thought, tapping her chin. Meanwhile, she'd already come to a decision hours ago. "While you weren't what I'd planned for, I am ready to make sacrifices." He had an intriguing honor, an excellent appearance, and a lack of a sycophant attitude or alpha male jerkiness that she liked.

"Sacrifices?" He practically choked on the word. "What have you sacrificed exactly?"

"I'd hoped for at least an admiral of a fleet. But you're still young, which means we can arrange for promotion."

"What if I like being a first mate?" He glared at her.

"Then you'll like being a captain even better."

"You can't decide my future."

Shutting off the holoscreen, she shifted to sit on the bed and fix him with a gaze. "Actually, I can. As my husband, there are now certain expectations of you."

"Your expectations can suck it."

She didn't recoil at the words. She'd have to get used to her husband's more profane manner of speaking. In some ways, it reminded her of Father when he forgot himself and reverted to his youthful method of speech.

"You will conform to your duties."

"And if I don't?"

"I wouldn't recommend it."

"Or you'll kill me, is that it?" He snorted. "Go ahead and try, princess."

"Me? Attack you?" This time she giggled. "Don't be silly. A lady doesn't conduct violence herself. I have my own guard to fight for me."

"I don't see any guards here," he remarked, stepping closer, his expression dark.

"Everyone on this ship is a possible soldier."

"And you think they'll kill me?" he queried.

"Make the right offer and people will kill anyone." A lesson taught by her father.

"Not everyone can be bought, princess." He hooked his thumbs into the waistband of his pants. "Captain says your father will probably be peeved about the wedding."

"He'll come around." Eventually. She might have to convince her father to keep Damon alive. Which was why she'd worked on a list of reasons he'd make her a good husband. Thus far, other than being pretty, he wasn't doing so great. "Just make me happy and I'm sure everything will be fine."

"What if I'm unhappy?" he grumbled, spinning from her and suddenly displaying a lot of flesh as he removed his shirt. The broadness of his back captivated, as did the delineation of his muscles.

She looked away. A Dkar follower practiced modesty even amongst members of the same sex. Staring at an unclothed male was wrong.

Was wrong being the key thing here.

I'm married. He's my husband. Which meant she could stare as much as she wanted—and even touch.

"Did it ever occur to you to use this marriage to your advantage?" she asked, rising from the bed. Because she'd sure as hell thought of a few ways it would work for her.

"Excuse me if I don't see one." He turned around as he pulled a softer shirt over his frame, hiding his luscious skin and the toned ridges of his muscles.

She drew closer to him, drawn despite his prickly words. "You don't seem to realize that you now have access to a fortune. To connections. You can become anything you want. A man of leisure. Business. Power. Even the admiral of your own fleet." With her at his side, a first lady of the galactic skies.

"What if I don't want to? What if I'm happy serving on this ship?"

Her nose wrinkled. "You'd rather work under

someone?" What an odd concept. Everyone wanted to be on top. The person everyone else bowed to.

"I happen to enjoy my position. I like seeing new places and things. I get to go on adventures. Meet people. Why the fuck would I give that up?"

"You could still have those things as captain of your own ship. Wouldn't you like to have your own command?"

"Don't you mean headache?" He grimaced. "No thanks. You should see the stupid shit Jameson goes through with the crew. Let someone else deal with the headaches."

This complete lack of motivation flummoxed her. "Don't you have any goals?"

"Yup. At the moment, my goal is getting some sleep. If you're done yapping, I'm going to bed."

He brushed past her, not close enough to touch, and yet the heat of his passing touched her skin and sent a shiver coursing through her.

He crawled onto the bed, grumbling something about, "Fucking bonbon blanket." Then he snuggled under the covering and said, "Lights out."

The room went dark, and there she stood, on her wedding night, clearly not about to be deflowered. Not exactly how she'd pictured it.

"Lights on." Brilliance illuminated the room. "Perhaps I wasn't clear before—"

"Lights off."

Pitch-black. "I am not done talking to you. Lights on."

"Lights off. And computer, only allow verbal commands by me in this room."

He had not just done that. "You can't do that. I am your wife."

"According to you. I didn't sign anything."

"You said the words."

"Do you have a witness?"

"The seal witnessed."

"I am pretty sure I can find a lawyer who knows someone who does auditory emotional forensics to say I sounded coerced."

Why was he being so stubborn? "This marriage is binding."

"We'll see what a judge says."

The mere fact that he didn't want her firmed her resolve to keep him. "You can't pretend it didn't happen."

He didn't reply.

"Damon?" Logistically, she knew he was still in the room with her, yet the lack of light played tricks on her mind. Perhaps she was alone in the room. She couldn't even hear him breathe. "Damon, you can't ignore me."

The silence stretched, and she took a step in the direction of the bed. Hit something hard enough to draw a yelp and send her tumbling to the floor.

Tears stung her eyes. Why had her life gotten so difficult as of late? All she'd wanted was a nice abduction by a halfway decent power-hungry male. A nice palace. Maybe a vacation place on a tropical planet.

Nothing was going according to plan. Especially

the part where her husband hated her. Which meant he'd have to die and she'd have to tempt a new husband, and yet she'd had the hardest time getting one in the first place. Damn her father for being over-protective and ruining her marital chances. *Sniffle.*

"Ah for fuck's sake." Hands gripped her and yanked her onto the bed, tucking her under a blanket warm from a body. His body.

"Does this—"

"Sleep, princess. Or I'll shove you out of this bed."

Given the bed was warm and soft and exciting, even if a certain male body moved to the other side, she elected to shut her lips.

She also closed her eyes and managed to sleep.

What she didn't expect was how she woke up. Splayed across Damon's body, wantonly pressing herself to him. Her leg draped over his lower half. Her palm flat against his chest. Her head tucked against his shoulder. His hand stroking her butt.

About time he acted as he should.

With a pleased grin, she flung herself onto her back and exclaimed, "I'm ready."

CHAPTER 5

"Ready for what?" he asked. For his part, he was ready to fuck. What guy wouldn't be? He'd just woken up with a hard-on, partially caused by a need to urinate, but also because he had a woman groping him.

However, while he was good to go, he doubted she was. For one thing, she'd just woken up and he'd not touched her. Except for her ass. It seemed only fair he got to rub something since she took advantage of him while he slept. But women required more than a little butt rub to get their sexual engine purring.

"I am ready for my deflowering."

The words froze him. Panic quickly followed. "Deflowering? You're a virgin."

"Not for long," she sang.

"No."

"What do you mean no? We are married. Consummation is required."

He clung to that word. Required. "In other words, if we don't have sex, the marriage isn't valid."

"Are you still trying to find a way to escape?" Her exasperation emerged loud and clear. "I told you, death is the only way out."

Rather than reply, he rolled out of bed. "Lights on." They illuminated, partially dimmed to alleviate any shock to his system. He should have left them off because he got quite the jolt when he looked over at Michonne.

Her hair had freed itself from whatever intricate design she'd had it in. Loose waves of it tumbled over her shoulders. The robe she'd gone to bed in the night before had obviously been shed during the night because she only wore a thin gown. A short one that rode up high enough that the leg she'd draped over him was bare. He'd felt it in that exposed strip between his shirt and pants.

Without the artifice of before, she'd lost some of her cool glamour. Fresh creamy skin with a hint of freckles across her nose, naturally long lashes, but a lighter brown in color. Pink lips currently pursed.

He glanced away and keyed in a code for some workout clothes. While he waited for the replicator to create them—because making clothes rather than storing and washing made more sense, especially since the dirty items were recycled to make new—he entered the washroom. Shut the door. It didn't help him forget who was on the other side.

She waited for him when he emerged. Wearing her

robe at least, her hair pulled into a bun at the base of her neck.

"Avoid it now, if you must. But as my husband, you will eventually come to me for your conjugal rights."

A good thing he faced the replicator chute because she might have seen the heat in his cheeks. "I don't need you to get my rocks off."

"While I'm not familiar with a rock technique, I do, however, feel I should mention at this time that your seal precludes you from indulging in full coitus with any biological entities apart from myself."

He whirled, clutching his clothes to this chest. "Excuse me?"

"The mark ensures fidelity."

"Which means what? I'll die if I touch another woman?"

"No. But you will find yourself extremely discomfited and unable to perform."

He looked down at his groin then back at her. "What did you do to my penis?"

"Nothing. The seal causes a chemical reaction on a vascular level if you attempt coitus with someone other than me."

"Whatever happened to trust?"

"It was betrayed too many times, so safeguards were put in place."

"The more I hear about your religion and culture, the more I'm thinking dying might be easier," he grumbled. The shock of knowing he truly was stuck with one woman just made him ornery.

"Am I truly that hideous to you?" The pompousness he'd already gotten used to gave way to a soft vulnerability.

He almost fell for it. "Are you seriously going to play a player?"

"Actually, I am being serious. Why are you so against us being together?"

"Apart from the fact we're strangers and have nothing in common?"

"Most successful marriages are arranged ones."

"If they're successful because you don't allow divorce, then I'd say your information is flawed."

Her lips quirked. "Actually, this comes from an observation of many cultures, which was part of the reasoning for the foundation of the Dkar religion."

"Just because you claim arranged marriages work out doesn't mean I believe it. And let's not forget the small percentage that don't."

"Perhaps they would have if both parties tried."

Her determination to be married frightened. "You can't expect me to just reverse a lifetime of expectations."

"Perhaps if you saw some of the benefits, you'd be less hesitant." She moved toward him, the sway of her hips riveting. She stopped in front of him and met his gaze with a tilted chin. "I promise we'll be very compatible."

He didn't have to ask in what way because she showed him. She stood on tiptoe and brushed a kiss over his lips. A light touch. Her hand curled around his nape to draw him nearer for a deeper embrace where her mouth tugged his, caressing the top and bottom with a sensuality that saw him unconsciously gripping her around the waist. Tugging her closer. Giving in...

Argh. *Don't let her fool you.*

He pulled away.

She cupped his cheeks to pull him back. Being a male, and a weak one, he didn't fight it.

"We shouldn't do this," he mumbled between kisses.

"I think we should do more." She slid her hand down, tracing the firm outline of his muscled arms then over to his waist, his buttocks. She gripped and pushed against him.

This time his erection was one hundred percent because of her.

She cupped him, and he hissed. "What are you doing?"

"Touching you." Said in an isn't-it-obvious kind of way.

"I thought you were a virgin." Didn't that mean innocent? Yet how many innocents acted so wantonly?

"Part of my lessons included that of eroticism and the many techniques to achieve favorable intercourse, important elements for a strong marriage bed. I've practiced in the holodecks for this moment," she admitted as she left soft nibbles along the ridge of his jaw.

The words penetrated. "Odd choice of lessons for a virgin." If it was true. The very idea terrified him—

while, at the same time, roused something deeply primal within.

"I was taught to not indulge in unmarried coitus. I was waiting for my husband." She bit the tip of his chin and whispered, "Waiting for you."

If ever there were words to make a man want to throw a woman onto a bed and slam into her body, she'd just used them.

The urge to claim her, to make her his, rode him hard. And as her husband, it was fully his right.

I'm her husband.

Shit.

The shock of it hit him again, and he had to push away from her. From the situation. "I've got to go. I always meet doc and the boys for some morning exercise." He didn't wait for a reply. Didn't look at her either lest he succumb to her allure and end up buried balls deep.

Exiting the room, he half expected her to follow, hence his stiff shoulders until he entered the holodeck he kept permanently reserved every morning at this time.

Being at space for long periods of time meant needing a means of entertainment and exercise. The holodeck provided both. In the antechamber, he took a moment to strip and put on gym clothes he still gripped that held the appearance of vintage twenty-first-century style. The shorts brightly colored with an odd symbol on the side, symbolic of the start of the Nike Galactic Corporation. They'd moved out of clothing centuries ago into space travel. Now their swoosh signature was how they built their ships.

Dressed, he palmed the panel to enter the holodeck itself, transformed into a space meant to play basketball, the ancient kind before the use of tiered nets and anti-grav shoes.

The floor took on the appearance of a driveway, the kind that used to house old combustion engine vehicles on wheels. Talk about ancient technology. Hover ability was the most basic mode of transportation nowadays. On some planets humans discovered, even the animals had ways to get around that didn't involve touching the ground.

Ivan and Karson were already there, dodging around the double-wide driveway. Ivan lunging to block as Karson slipped around him, leapt and dunked the ball into a net suspended from a replica holographic nineteen-nineties garage.

One day, if he ever did retire, he was going to build what became known in the nineteen-nineties and early two-thousands as a cookie-cutter home on a piece of land. He might try and recreate the nostalgic days gone by. Maybe even see if he had enough credits to get one of the original combustion-belching cars.

"There's the married man." Karson spun around and smirked as he hit the ground, lazily reaching out to catch the bouncing orange sphere.

"Look at the face on him. Already he has the appearance of a husband." Ivan scrunched his features into a scowl that only served to deepen the one forming.

"Fuck off. This isn't funny."

"Nor very satisfying apparently," Karson noted, pitching him the ball. "What's the matter? Your new wife not like your mug?"

"You could try wearing a holomask of my face," Ivan offered.

"My wife likes my looks just fine." Damon winced even saying the word.

"Do you always look angry after sex?" Ivan asked.

"We haven't had sex." Yet.

Hold on. Never. This marriage wasn't real. No matter what everyone said.

"No wonder he's pissed."

"I am not pissed," he said, thrusting the ball at Ivan, who caught it with a laugh.

"If you say so."

"Shut up about my sex life and play." He lunged at Ivan and, for the next while, forgot his woes as he played. The exertion did much to revive him and expel some frustration.

But once they were done and in the cleansing units, the dilemma returned to plague him. He leaned his face over the stall door as the laser units passed over his body, destroying all dirt and sweat particles. "What do you know of the Dkar religion?"

Karson whistled. "I've heard about it. That's for the rich folk."

Which probably explained why he didn't know much about it. "Is it strict?"

"Wouldn't really know. It's not openly taught. What I do know is it's part alien and part ancient-Earth Scientology. Once you're part of it, there's no getting out."

"Not exactly reassuring." He wasn't one to worship at altars to false idols.

"Maybe you should have thought of that before marrying," was Ivan's riposte as he joined in.

"It was spur of the moment."

"Did you at least get her name?"

"Her name is Michonne." Something or other.

"Michonne what?"

"I don't know." Because it wasn't in the file. Jameson had only given him the barest outline. Which should have been fine if the woman hadn't tied him down.

Karson let out a low chuckle. "I can't believe you married someone and you don't even know her last name."

"It wasn't like I had a choice."

"Is that what you're going to tell everyone? That she's your accidental wife?" Ivan asked. "That probably won't go over well."

"If what I know of the Dkar is true, she'll be a widow fairly quick," was Karson's more ominous addition.

"What else did you hear?" He turned and gripped the edge of the stall to better see his friend.

"Just that the Dkar don't like those outside their social circle marrying in without proper vetting."

"If they don't like it, then why not kick her out?" And in the process, kick him out.

"You don't just quit the Dkar," snorted Ivan.

"How would you know?"

Ivan, a bulky blond fellow, faced away but still replied. "All I know is rumors. Rumors that say you have to be approved to join. Given how rich I imagine your new wife's father is, he won't like her marrying a commoner."

"I've got money."

"Not that kind of money. But don't worry, I have a plan," Ivan declared. "We'll announce to your wife that we're lovers and that she must run before I kill her in a jealous fit."

"As if anyone would believe I'd sleep with you. We both know Gerome would skin me alive." Gerome being Ivan's partner.

"He would. The man gets so jealous. But the love-making after a fight..." Ivan grinned and winked. "Well worth it."

Karson groaned. "Always with the games. Can't the pair of you just have normal sex? Like a normal couple?"

Damon snickered as Ivan uttered an emphatic, "No."

"I wonder who her father is," Damon murmured aloud. Because Jameson never said. Just gave him the basics, along with her name, first only, and a picture.

"Why don't you ask her?"

Because asking her meant talking to her. Looking at her. Being tempted by a woman who'd saved her maidenhead for her husband. A woman who wanted to be seduced.

Heading to the bridge, and his duties, he resolved to find out more before confronting her again. Once he did get a name, a name that punched him in the face, he delayed that meeting to get drunk. Really, really drunk, because finding out he was married to the daughter of one of the universe's biggest crime lords was enough to throw him off-kilter. He needed booze to numb himself to the dilemma he found himself in.

His new wife didn't appreciate his inebriated state, or so he assumed, because she met him with a yell and tried to clobber him. She missed, the boot bouncing off his stomach.

"My turn," he slurred before reaching for her. But he misjudged, or she moved, and he hit the bed face-first.

"Mmm. Soft." Comfy. Zzz...

CHAPTER 6

MICHI STARED at the snoring shape of her husband, passed out drunk on the bed.

She planted her hands on her hips and glared. "Jerk."

He didn't move. Or apologize.

"Do you have any idea what you did?"

He stayed silent except for some rumbly snores.

"You left." Left without saying when he'd return. Without a goodbye. Nothing. Left her in a room where she couldn't do a damn thing because he'd made the room only obedient to him.

He didn't drop to a knee and beg her forgiveness.

"Do you have any idea what it's like being locked in a room by yourself?" It meant pounding on a door, a door no one opened. Stupid soundproof space ships. "It means not being able to ask the computer to play music or a movie." Or calling her daddy and whining about her new husband. The jerk who'd left her all alone after refusing coitus, as was her right as his wife.

He snored.

It said he didn't care. She lost her ladylike mind for a moment. "Damn you." She hit him. Again and again. He didn't flinch, move, or do anything, and she suddenly stopped.

What am I doing?

Acting crazy that was what. She'd been knocked off balance and needed to regroup.

How am I supposed to do that? With him passed out, she was still unable to get out of this room. And while the replicator worked by simple button press, she wasn't sure where she'd go if she did escape this room.

In her culture, you were either married or living with family waiting for marriage. Single people of any age had no rights.

I'd have some as a widow, though. But only if she wasn't caught. Her religion had strict punishments for those that killed their partners without just cause or permission.

She stared at the sleeping shape of her husband. A man who'd gone through a culture shock, a man who did desire her even if he fought it. A man Father would hate. But who intrigued her.

She sat on the edge of the bed and ran a finger down his back. Firm flesh encased by fabric. She ran her fingers to the edge of the shirt and slipped under it. Hot skin met her fingertips, and she stilled.

This was wrong. The touching while he slept. The lusting. She snatched her hand away and bit her lip.

He's my husband.

Barely.

She needed to change that if this marriage was to survive her father's arrival. She had no doubt that would be soon.

Kneeling, she removed his footwear. Tugged off his trousers and did her best to ignore the perfection of his bare buttocks. She tried removing his shirt, but he proved too heavy.

Yank, push, shove. All she did was cause herself exertion and annoyance. She paused, kneeling on the bed beside him. "Dammit, can't you cooperate with one thing?"

He opened one eye. "Wassa matter, princess?" he slurred.

"I need your shirt off."

"Okay." He tugged if off and then rolled to his side, giving her an eyeful. She turned her head, a heated blush in her cheeks. The holodeck simulations might have shown her what to expect, but faced with the real thing, she felt suddenly inexperienced and shy.

"Come here," he ordered, squinting in the dim light he'd left on all day. He crooked a finger. "Come here, wifey poo." Crooned with a crooked smile.

"As you wish, husband." She shimmied out of her skirt to his appreciative gaze. Then got stuck a moment in her shirt trying to take it off. She tossed it to the side and thrust out her chest, only to realize he snored again.

"You have to be joking." Why did this man persist in making this difficult? Well, he wouldn't win, not this time. She climbed into bed, took a deep breath, then lay beside him, as naked as he was. Inched closer and closer until their skins touched, then froze.

Actually, more like she burned. The contact stole her breath. Then she couldn't breathe even if she wanted to, given the heavy arm he threw over her. He held her tight. Warmed her from head to toe and in a few places that made her cheeks burn.

How she fell asleep, she couldn't have said, but she did.

Next thing she knew, a hand cupped her breast, a thumb brushed over her nipple. A hard rod pressed against her backside, and her husband hummed as he nuzzled her hair.

Such small things and yet far more intense than the holodeck ever led her to imagine. Her lips parted in a soft sigh as his lips found her neck and slid over it. A trembling moan as he pinched the tip of her breast.

"I shouldn't do this," he murmured suddenly, pulling his hand away. Only to have her grab it and bring it back. She placed it on her breast.

"Touch me. Please." She didn't demand or order, but asked.

"This will make things complicated," he murmured, the words brushing the skin of her neck.

"It's already complicated. Why can't we find something pleasurable in it?" she asked, dragging his hand lower then sucking in a breath when his fingers brushed over her mound.

He cupped her, bold and heated strength holding her most private part. She closed her eyes and held her breath, fearful that any sound, even a movement, would send him fleeing.

"Why are we naked?" he asked, his hand motionless.

"Because it feels good." It did. She wiggled against him, and he uttered a soft groan.

"You shouldn't do that."

"Why not?" She squirmed again.

The hand cupping her squeezed. She gasped. His lips touched the lobe of her ear.

"It's evil to tempt a man."

"I'd say it's more evil to keep teasing me." She wiggled, giving herself a thrill as his fingers rubbed.

"Is this what you want?" His dragged a finger along the slit of her sex, and she drew in a shuddering breath. "You don't have to answer, do you? I can feel it." He rubbed his slick finger against her clitoris, and she moaned. His words rumbled against her as he continued to rub. "I thought I was dreaming when I woke up with you snuggled against me."

And she thought she dreamed now, his heavenly touch making her shiver in pleasure.

"You are really here, though. Wet and ready." He inserted part of a finger in her, and she tensed. "Tight. So fucking tight."

He rolled her onto her back and poised himself over her. She stared at him, frightened and yet excited. Aroused and ready.

She went to drape her arms around him, but he shook his head. "Oh no you don't, princess." She might have protested except he chose to work his way down her body, starting with her jaw, then a slide of his lips down her neck.

He reached her collarbone and nipped her. She arched.

Every part of her throbbed with awareness.

His lips latched onto a nipple, and she cried out as her sex clenched.

"Damon." She sighed his name, and he growled.

"Dammit, princess, when you say it like that..." He never finished his sentence, choosing to instead drag his lips down the silky skin of her belly, farther still to her mound.

Surely he wasn't about to... He did, and reading about it, seeing it on screen, and pretending on a holodeck did not do it justice.

The first swipe of his tongue and her hips arched off the bed.

He pinned her down for the second. Then she lost track of everything as ecstasy attacked her body. Made her cry out. Climax. Cry out some more.

When he finally poised himself atop her tingling body, the head of him ready to penetrate, she was more than ready.

A satisfied smile pulled her lips. "Take me."

"With pleasure." He began to push, the head of him spearing her, and she held her breath—

The computer interrupted. "First Mate Falkner, you are required on the bridge."

"Fuck."

CHAPTER 7

DAMON MUTTERED "FUCK" a few more times between rolling off Michonne's hot body, yanking on his pants, fabricating a new shirt, and doing a quick toiletry session. As he emerged from the ablutions room, it didn't help to see her rosy-cheeked in his bed, her hair spilling over her naked shoulders.

"You're leaving again?" she asked.

"You heard the computer. Work."

"Can you at least give me permission to exit your quarters?"

"What are you talking about?" Only as soon as he asked, he knew. "Shit, you couldn't leave the room yesterday. No wonder you were so mad. Fuck. I'm sorry. I didn't mean to do that. Computer, allow Michonne full access to my quarters."

"Thank you." The smile she gave him went right to his cock—his poor blue balls just sobbed.

"Uh." Yeah, that was what the smooth first mate

managed to say to the woman who'd come so gloriously on his tongue not that long before. The reminder didn't help his frustration situation.

Which might have explained his scowl when he entered the bridge to see the captain had called most of his senior crew, which meant him as first mate, as well as the second mate, who usually worked an opposing shift to Damon. Which suited Lazarine just fine. She preferred the nocturnal hours on board. Both majors were there, being the chief medical officer, Karson, and that of the environment, Ivan. Einstein rounded out their party, her petite body dwarfed by her seat, one of the rare cases where a human couldn't be fixed by modern medicine. Between her hybrid genes and being raised on a zero-gravity asteroid without access to the basics, Einstein never had a chance. But while her body might have crippled, her mind flourished.

The captain entered last. "I see everyone is here." Everyone except Crank. The captain let the cyborg get away with insubordination. Everyone did. Poor guy suffered.

Will I turn into Crank if I lose my wife? Probably not since she indicated he'd die soon after. Still, it did bring a moment of pause to wonder if she was right, that their arranged marriage could work and maybe he'd end up truly caring for her.

Aren't I already starting?

"Thanks for gathering. I wanted to talk to you before we land."

75

"Land where? We are still two days out from the way station." Damon frowned.

"We need to make a pit stop first. Here." Jameson waved his hand, and a holomap appeared. A pulsing red point drew the eye.

"You're taking us to La'zuun. Since when do you gamble?" asked Karson.

La'zuun was an asteroid that thrived on vices. Especially those frowned upon by most evolved societies. Yet even the most educated and intelligent retained a somewhat primal need for the taboo and the violent.

Places like La'zuun with its gambling, arena for bloodshed, and boudoirs for seduction—and pain— filled the void. And made great credits doing so. They were also dangerous places where the wrong bet or move could see someone playing the part of the next victim in the arena.

Given it was a place to relax, Damon asked, "Should we begin dividing the crew into away parties?"

"We won't be staying long enough for that."

An in-and-out affair. Damon cocked a brow. "Crew won't like that." Any docking time was considered sacrosanct. Even after centuries in space, humanity still required some kind of contact with the ground. To feel gravity, real gravity, tugging at them. Breathing real air.

"We can't stay long because we'll probably be coming out hot," Jameson advised, a swipe of his hand enlarging the planet. A green and blue ball. Once a derelict hunk of rock, floating alone around a star, it had been terra formed at great expense and turned into a playground.

Ivan grumbled, "Can you not delay whatever trouble you've got planned long enough to give the crew some deserved down time?"

"They'll get downtime when we hit the station in a few days," Jameson said.

More than one face sported a grimace. "Not exactly the same," Karson noted. "I have to agree with others. As chief medical officer, I do think the crew could use a few hours in a place with grass and trees and people other than those they're sick of."

"We have grass in the conservatory, and if they don't like the people here, then there's the holodeck. We can't stay." Jameson glared all around, but while they followed the man fiercely and loyally, none had gotten there by being pushovers. They didn't shrivel under his glare, and he sighed. "Fine. Twelve hours. No more. And make sure it's clear we're not staying. Anyone not on board at departure time will damned well stay behind."

"Aye, aye, captain." Damon snapped a salute.

Jameson smirked. "Years later and you still can't do it right. No wonder you flunked out of the academy." Being the galactic academy where the best and brightest of humanity's soldiers trained.

Damon thanked all the stars he'd not ended up shoehorned into an awful career. Shuttling dignitaries.

Dealing with colony problems. Getting killed in wars that didn't mean shit.

"Now that we've dealt with that, our next dilemma. The first mate's new wife."

Damon grimaced. "Do we have to drag that out now?"

"I think by now everyone knows about your accidental wedding." Jameson smirked. "But what you don't know is that poses some difficulties. First and foremost being the fact that her father sent me to rescue her and, instead, my first mate married her."

"Technically, she married me. I would have said no."

"Won't matter. You are her husband, and since you don't have a family name, planet, or army behind you, her father is going to be less than pleased."

"And what do you suggest I do about that?" Damon asked.

"Make her very, very happy."

"I can give you pointers if needed," Ivan remarked.

"Don't listen to the sausage fest," Einstein interjected. "Just be yourself."

"I thought we wanted him to succeed in making her happy," Karson noted.

Lazarine snickered. "Then he's screwed."

Jameson cleared his throat. "How about we let Damon figure out how to woo his wife on his own. I just want you to be aware in case we need to make a hasty departure when we do end up meeting with him. But I doubt that will be for a few days. In the meantime, I need you all ready for our upcoming La'zuun excursion."

"Going to tell us why we're here?" Karson asked.

"No."

"But you're pretty sure we will be leaving hot," Damon queried.

"Probably."

"Then I'd better warn Crank."

Except Crank already knew. Which left Damon with nothing much to do. Everyone was already hard at work. He'd made the rounds twice already. He couldn't avoid it anymore.

His room.

His wife.

What they'd started...

Why did he fear her? *You heard what the captain said. You need to make her happy.* It was a matter of life or death. Yet, the fact that he had to do it, had to make her the happiest woman alive, made him balk. What about what he wanted?

I want her.

Yes, he did, in the moment, for now. What about after they'd slept together? What about when they tired of each other? Surely their passion—even if ridiculously strong now—would fade.

It doesn't fade with everyone. There were examples of relationships that lasted everywhere he went. He knew of numerous couples on board the ship happy with their choice.

He knew just as many that were happier to split.

The door to his room loomed in front of him. Behind it, a future he'd never asked for but had to accept.

The hardship. Married to a gorgeous, rich woman. The horror.

I'm an idiot. Since he couldn't change things, he should embrace it. Embrace her. With his tongue. Again. Because she tasted so damned delicious.

He walked toward his door, which, recognizing him, slid open. "Princess, I'm home." Declared to an empty room.

Where the hell had his wife gone?

CHAPTER 8

HER HUSBAND ARRIVED WEARING a thunderous expression. Perched on a stool that could swivel, she quickly turned her back and pretended she never saw him. A coy game, but one she'd learned along with how to manage credits, a household, and more. Papa made sure all his daughters received a thorough education.

She faked a smile for the man talking *at* her. Not to her. He was much too self-involved for that.

He—Lieutenant Gower something or other—finally paused talking about his greatness when her husband growled, "Move away from my wife."

"Wife?" the man squeaked—apparently a trait among the crew—and fled.

"Well, that was rude," she remarked, taking a sip from the concoction someone had labeled a drink. More like the fluid used to strip the color from her nails when she tired of it.

"What the hell are you doing here?" He bore a scowl that didn't detract from his handsomeness at all.

"I am having a beverage. Care to join me?" She indicated the now vacant seat.

"No. You shouldn't be here."

Here being the hidden heart of the ship, known as Nexus by the crew, where the fun things occurred, such as needling her new husband. "I'm sorry, was I supposed to remain in our quarters? Perhaps waiting on my knees with your slippers in hand? Or am I simply not allowed to speak to anyone?"

"That's not what I meant."

"Then what did you mean, husband? Because it sounded as if you were forbidding me from socializing."

"Socialize, yes, but you can't flirt with other men."

Her brow arched as he inadvertently admitted his jealousy. "I didn't realize conversation was considered flirting now."

"It's not usually, however, Goweranski is a womanizer."

"The lieutenant was wasting his time then. I am a married woman."

"Which he obviously didn't realize." Damon scrubbed a hand through his hair. "We're going to have to find a way to make it understood you're off-limits."

"You wish to mark me unavailable? I guess we could tattoo my face. Perhaps invest in a flashing sign that I can carry about stating your ownership." She knew she teased, and yet she couldn't help it. This jealous side of him fascinated and excited.

"I was thinking more along the lines of a ring."

"A ring?" She looked at her bare fingers. "But that's so archaic." The use of rings had been a ritual employed by humans centuries ago and had long since been abandoned for other more permanent methods.

"I'm an old-fashioned guy."

"So I'm discovering. And will you also be wearing a ring to state your status?"

"You already marked me."

But not anywhere visible. Which meant the women ogling him across the room didn't yet realize he was unavailable. She placed her hand on his arm. "I hear we'll be making port shortly."

"Don't get too excited. We won't be there long."

"Are we docking for business?" she asked.

"Of a sort. I don't know the details, and even if I did, I couldn't tell you."

"Understandable. Still, it will be enjoyable to visit."

"No visiting for you. I'll have to go with the captain, which means you'll have to remain on board."

A frown creased her brow. "Am I not allowed off the ship without you as a chaperone?"

"Usually, yes, but you can't in this place. La'zuun is dangerous for women."

"You are not allowing any females to disembark?"

Judging by the tightness of his jaw, only she was forbidden. "Only you, because you're different."

"How am I different?" She leaned forward, drawn to this man. Fascinated by the way he treated her, one moment acting as if he didn't want anything to do with her, the next possessive. So very, very possessive.

"We don't yet know for sure if the Kanishqui commander has given up on you."

He'd be foolish to continue trying. She'd made her choice, and even if the commander killed Damon, as a widow, she'd have more choice in her next husband. "Surely he didn't follow us." They'd streaked a number of times, enough to lose him.

"We've seen no signs of pursuit, but we can't know if there are others who will be tempted by your wealth."

She waved a hand, dismissing his concern. "My marriage to you has made my abduction worthless. My only merit was in my ability to wed and confer my wealth and status. If anyone is in danger, it's you. Perhaps you should be locked away. For your protection of course," she teased.

"I don't need protection."

"Are you sure of that?" She stepped off the stool and stood close to him, so close her body couldn't help but heat, remembering his touch. The pleasure she'd felt at his hands and tongue were something she craved more of.

His arm curled around her waist and drew her near, pulling her up on tiptoe. "Do you need a lesson in my virility?"

He flirted with her, and she couldn't help but

smile. "Perhaps I do. Should we adjourn to our quarters that you might best instruct me?"

"Let's go."

He led her from the gathering place, his arm around her waist tantalizing her. Every so often they'd have to pause at a busy intersection, and he'd draw her close, tucking her into his warmth, not saying anything, to her at least. He briefly acknowledged the crew they encountered, his words to them short, almost terse. Dare she say, impatient.

Finally, they reached his room and its privacy. The door no sooner closed than she was pushed against it, his mouth finding hers for fervent embrace. They only managed that single passionate kiss before the ship announced the crew needed to get ready for docking.

"Fuck me," he groaned, leaning his forehead against hers.

She could understand his disappointment, especially since his departure left her aching.

But he wouldn't be gone forever. Damon had said it himself. They would only be at this planet for a short while. She just had to show patience. Await his return. Simple enough.

She spent the first few minutes tidying their room. Recycling garments. Spreading the blanket on the bed. Pacing. Lying on the bed.

How much longer? A glance at the time showed they'd barely just arrived.

Sigh.

Michi meant to behave and do as Damon asked.

Defying his orders wouldn't bring them closer, and he was right. There was still a possible danger to her. Not many would yet know of her marriage.

Yet, all her good intentions went out the door when the communicator in the room chimed with a message for Michonne from the planet. A message she couldn't ignore.

CHAPTER 9

"Nice place," Damon murmured to the captain as they disembarked from the ship.

Unlike previous versions of the pleasure resort, La'zuun was truly a paradise. Long gone were the days when the vice lords ran their operation on a barren asteroid. Only the most long-lived remembered the Maestro A'Diabbloh who ran his operation with decadence and mind control until the day a Rhomanii prince destroyed it.

Nowadays Madame Papyon played hostess to those who visited the vice planet. She even greeted them personally, the four breasts of her voluptuous upper body hugged by the finest silks. Her serpentine tresses, a bright shade of green, were lively and snapped at any that came too close. The hem of her gown undulated as her sinuous lower body moved along the smooth polished floors of the arrival building. The spaceport was gigantic—white stone and glass and technology. It had to be high tech to handle all the various ships that came to play.

"Kobrah, darling," Madame Papyon gushed. "It's been agessss." She rolled her S's, the hiss of them flicking off her forked tongue while her two slitted yellow eyes regarded the captain with avarice.

"You are looking as delicious as ever," the captain remarked, taking her hand and kissing the top of it. A modification she'd had done, given her kind lacked true appendages.

An artificial pinkness flushed her gray/green skin. "Such a flirt. To what do I owe this pleasssure?"

"Can't a man stop in to see a friend? I was passing by and thought we could share a drink."

"What a sssplendid idea."

Could anyone else read the falseness in their conversation? Damon knew for a fact the captain didn't like or trust Madame Papyon at all. Just like he knew they'd gone out of their way to come here. What game did his captain play?

Whatever it was, Captain Jameson shot a look back at Damon and said, "Make sure the crates I ordered are delivered. Then take a few minutes for yourself. Check out the market. See if something catches your eye for the new wife."

In other words, make himself scarce and keep an eye open. What did Jameson think he'd find? The man held his secrets close to his chest. Always had. But Damon knew enough to realize they were here for a reason. Was that reason the twelve crates delivered to the *Moth*? Sealed tight and without any kind of shipping label, anything could have been inside. Although, judging by the fact Crank stirred himself from engineering to oversee their delivery, he'd bet it had something to do with the ship's engines and power cells.

"Is this going to fix our secondary power source?" he asked as Crank spent a moment by each crate staring at them.

"Yep."

"Why didn't the captain tell us we were stopping to grab supplies for you?" Why the big mystery?

"This isn't the reason why we stopped. Simply a bonus," Crank noted. "Now if we're done wasting time yapping, I've got work to do." The implication being unlike some.

"Have fun unpacking. I'm going to check on the crew."

While overseeing the delivery, Damon had made sure the crewmembers chosen by lottery to disembark were reminded not to miss their departure time. The captain had been adamant on that point, which meant they'd probably be leaving hot.

The last group had departed, leaving the vessel with a skeleton crew of about fifty. A ship their size could carry several hundred. A small mobile town with people serving all kinds of roles because flying the *Moth* was only part of it.

With his task complete, he had two choices, wander the planet, perhaps pick up some intelligence or goods.

Or...

He eyed the ship with its glossy gray exterior. Inside was his wife. A wife who waited on him.

A wife he'd much rather see than a raucous marketplace.

However, the captain had more or less given an order that he remain available and alert. And then there was the memory of the lieutenant who thought he could flirt with Michonne. That made him realize he did need to do something to advertise the fact she wasn't available.

His tongue ran over the emblem on the inside of his lip. Each time he thought of his wife, he felt a spurt of warmth. A thrill.

Was it the mark making him experience those sensations or something else? Perhaps the fact he didn't mind being married to her?

Would she want her own symbol of their binding? Something she could rub and remind herself of him.

She'd not scoffed when he mentioned a ring, and the marketplace was the right place to shop for one. He'd be solving several problems at once.

With one last look at the *Moth*, Damon took long strides and managed to make it onto a tram just leaving for the city core. He slung his body into a seat and made himself comfortable as the doors swished shut.

A slight lurch and they were off. The tram rode an invisible track in the sky and provided visitors with a rapid yet beautiful ride to the city. While they travelled ridiculously fast, the holowindows made it appear as if they took a leisurely ride and portrayed stunning vistas lush with orange grass, the gray boles of the trees smooth and perfectly round, the pillow-top tips of them a fluffy white cloud. Wild animals danced among the fronds. Water splashed over scenic waterfalls.

Very relaxing, especially since everyone had their own seat, a plush armchair type that cradled the body no matter the shape. It molded to them for a comfortable ride.

When the tram arrived, a melodious chime rang, and chattering excitedly, the entities on board disembarked. Humans, bipedals that closely resembled them, and other aliens that shared nothing in common with water-based creatures. The universe had a lot of chitinous sorts as well as tentacled.

Emerging from the tram, Damon looked around to get his bearings. While he had been to La'zuun before, each time the vista changed. To keep things fresh and exciting, the downtown marketplace was constantly moving as old sections were demolished and rebuilt. The ultimate tourist destination knew how to maintain a rotation so that guests were never put out.

The majority of those he rode with on the tram split left and right. Gambling one way. Sex and violence the other. He and a few others chose straight ahead, the marketplace being their destination.

It amused him to see the current rendition resembled an ancient bazaar on Earth, the kind held in the sandy cities of Egypt. The buildings were made to appear constructed of ancient stone while the fronts sported bright awnings and, under them, wooden tables spread with wares.

Food vendors worked from rickety carts, spewing mouthwatering smells as they basted meat over coal fires. Fake, of course. No one used real pollution-creating methods of combustion anymore.

The entire thing looked utterly authentic, and for all he knew, some of it was, painstakingly bought and shipped and rebuilt on this alien planet. But for all it seemed real, he knew it was but a façade. La'zuun was a giant stage to give the customer the full experience.

But like any other amusement park, he could enjoy it. He wasn't alone in finding pleasure in the ancient bazaar setting. As he strolled, he noted some of the crew amongst the crowd browsing the wares. Even waved to a few. Everywhere he looked he saw smiles, a pleasure planet doing its job and pleasing its guests.

The sound of chatter filled the air and yet couldn't be understood. The vocal dampeners ensured privacy in public, allowing people to converse.

Crowded around the first few vendors were those looking to eat. He was tempted to join them. The scent of that meat, skewered with some kind of vegetable, was redolent with spice. His mouth watered. He looked away and noticed pastries, fluffy and stuffed with incredible things.

On his way back, he'd purchase some. Nothing beat real and fresh food. Throat parched meant he didn't resist a drink. He snared a refreshing beverage made from real crushed fruit as opposed to the replicated kind. No alcohol. He was on duty.

One last thing did distract him and cause him to put out too many credits, but how could he resist the bag of oranges? Authentic ones from Earth that cost a fortune but were delicious.

Damon had a runner—a paid La'zuun employee in purple and gold livery—take it back to the ship. A free service. The planet did its best to ensure people would shop unencumbered. An empty-handed guest was more likely to buy more.

Farther into the market, the crowd thinned as the more luxurious items prevailed. Rare fabrics such as the gossamer threads from the At'lantius arachnids, which, when woven, could stop even a direct burst of plasma fire. Extremely rare and valuable since the spidery race only allowed a controlled amount in the market at any one time.

There were premade fashions, the latest in galactic wear, plus tailors on site should an outfit need adjusting. Did you happen to be a pure descended human with only two breasts? They could modify that dress or remove the slack in the groin for the men who possessed only one penis rather than two.

Artifacts abounded, from strange silvery shards that appeared to be broken parts of something larger to items he recognized from Earth. Old Earth. Like a two-wheeled contraption called a bike. And an ugly doll in a flimsy paper box with a plastic shield called a Cabbage Patch Kid—worth a planetary fortune.

Other things were truly alien such as the single black spike that hummed and the thing in a cage that was not a bird or lizard—but something in between—and had an impressive array of teeth it showed when it sang.

Amongst these goods Damon found the jewelers. The display of valuables more sedate than the others. Here they tended to showcase a few items, truly allowing their beauty to shine. The pendant necklace with the swirling orb, a pocket universe that could act as a purse. The matching collars with the filigree that would penetrate the skin and truly bond a couple. A little too much for him.

A golden butt plug with a ruby tip. Again, not his style. Nor were the pincer clamps for nipples and other sensitive parts. The cock ring got a second look, but that was for his and her pleasure, not for showing off.

He finally had to ask. "Do you have other types of rings?"

The vendor, a shrunken fellow, the folds of his red skin hanging, looked him in the face and lower. "Looking for a smaller size?"

The implication didn't have the ability to embarrass. Not anymore. As the vendor belonged to a race called the Gonnfl, it meant his cock—actually his entire body—could inflate to splendid sizes. The males and females puffing up and bouncing off each other as part of their mating ritual.

"As a matter of fact, I need a much smaller size." Before the shopkeeper could give him a look of pity,

Damon held up his hand. "Something to fit a finger. A woman's finger. Something fancy. With a good-sized stone."

"One moment." The shopkeeper disappeared into his store and eventually returned with a large box. Larger than expected.

Damon frowned. Especially once he opened it. "That thing is bigger than her head." The giant red stone had smaller stones attached to it to act as buoys to ensure the rock could be lifted. But it was technically a ring. A peek under showed the little loop for the finger.

"That's not quite what I was hoping for. Do you have something smaller? More vintage. I want an engagement ring, not..." He waved his hand. "That."

The vendor's eyes—all over his visage—widened. "You seek a mating relic from Earth. It is your lucky day, sir. We have one of those. Just came in."

It proved to be exactly what Damon had imagined, and the price reflected it.

"I will not promise you my first born," Damon snapped.

"What about promising the first female of your line to be engaged with a male member of mine?" The Gonnfl rubbed his hands, and parts of him began to inflate with excitement.

"Let's keep this transaction to credits or non-living goods only."

It took much haggling before Damon finally got the ring price to a place where he didn't feel as if his ass needed a kiss better. His savings, though? They took a big hit.

He'd no sooner sent the ring off to the ship than he heard a commotion.

Damon emerged from the store to see guards, their uniforms a stark black against all the color, invading the marketplace, checking inside every store, stopping anyone with a head covering and making them show themselves.

When the soldiers neared him, he asked, "Who are you looking for?"

"None of your business," was the grunted reply by the rather porcine fellow, his short tusks blunted at the tips. And to think their ancestors used to pride themselves on the length and sharpness. Then again, once upon a time, humans had five toes. The fifth one being utterly useless and only rarely appearing in babies nowadays.

The soldier moved on, and Damon kept watch long enough to realize they probably wouldn't find what they sought here. Whoever it was, was obviously worth a pretty penny because Madame Papyon didn't usually let anything mar the pleasure experience.

About to head back to the *Moth*, Damon noticed the soldiers stop someone in a blue-hooded robe. Which in and of itself wasn't unusual. It was the person wearing it that had him cursing.

"What the fuck is she doing here?"

And where did those soldiers think they were taking his wife?

Damon didn't even think twice; he began following them. The question of why Michonne had disobeyed and left the ship was something he'd deal with later.

Taking a side street, the soldiers marched Michonne away from the city center. Away from everything public.

He did his best to stay close behind, wondering how he'd extricate her. Because there was no way they were keeping his wife, and this didn't even have anything to do with the mark in his mouth.

This was about them taking Michonne from him. Of laying hands—er, hooves—on her.

A husband had a few lines. At least from what he'd gleaned during his life. Don't cheat. Don't gamble. And don't let anyone do anything to your wife. It was a matter of pride.

He should also add that, in this day and age, the rules also applied for women. She was expected to be ready and willing to come to his aid. A marriage was an equal partnership. And this was where all the equal rights laws could get tricky. Some would say, let her save herself, she was strong and capable.

However, anyone who'd ever fought a battle knew that sometimes you could use a helping hand. Not to mention he couldn't exactly give Michonne shit—and maybe a sensual spanking—for leaving the *Moth* if she wasn't on the ship.

The soldiers led her through a maze of alleys linking the public places to the pleasure zones. Behind the scenes where the tourists couldn't see.

Oddly enough, no one questioned his right to be there. Not yet, but Damon knew cameras watched him, hoping he'd do something epic—and possibly stupid—that they could sell to the galactic entertainment stations.

Actors just never managed the same emotion and reality of those caught on a candid camera. The oddest individuals could become stars.

The guards took his wife through a matte gray door, the dull metal not even reflecting light. He stood outside for a moment. Looked up. Could almost hear his captain say, "Do you have to do it?"

And since he could emphatically reply, "Yeah, I do," he pulled open the door and entered. Went through a kitchen prep area where gray-faced beings glanced in his direction but didn't say a thing. He meant to take his time and not rush in. Then Michonne screamed, and he kicked in the door to the next room!

CHAPTER 10

THIS IS UNEXPECTED. Michonne gaped at her husband as he stood, fists raised, glowering, then confused.

"How did you find me?" she gasped. She'd not even known where to go when she'd left the ship. Good thing those soldiers she found in the market place offered to guide her.

"Get behind me. I'll figure a way out of here." Damon still had his fists clenched, ready to fight. Because he'd yet to realize she wasn't in danger. Currently. That could change rather quickly.

She laughed. "Lunilla, I'd like you to meet my husband. First Mate Damon Faulkner. Damon, this is my sister Lunilla." A sister who looked nothing at all like Michi with her platinum locks piled in intricate loops atop her head, her very voluptuous figure, and electric blue eyes, a modification she claimed made her see in the dark.

"Sister?" he repeated, his hands falling to his sides.

"Yes, sister. She's the reason I left the ship. She somehow found out I was on board and sent me a message that she was here." Actually, the note bragged about the fact that Lunilla had birthed her latest child, another son to inherit, and as a reward, her husband had brought her to La'zuun for a pampering vacation. But it was the postscript that sent her hustling to see Lunilla.

"He's your husband?" Lunilla murmured. "So this is the man Father is going to hate." Her sister's gaze tracked Damon head to toe. "He's attractive. Pity he isn't at least a captain."

"He could be," Michi staunchly defended.

"It might not be too late. Mutiny now and have him take control. Also, be sure to get pregnant and maybe, just maybe, you can convince Father not to kill him. Unless you'd rather be rid of him. Say the word."

"Luni!" Michi gasped, her shock loud. "He's my husband."

"Only because he saved you before that Kanishqui lord could claim you. Pity. I hear he owns two planets."

"Marriage isn't always about more stuff," Michi huffed. "It should be about other things, too."

"Like?" Lunilla sounded genuinely puzzled.

"Like..." Love or affection would be mocked, as would lust. What did that leave? "Compatible taste in cake."

"You'd base your future on cake?" Lunilla smirked. "Go right ahead. When you die, my portion of the family treasure will get larger."

Michi sucked in a breath. "That was cold."

"But true, little sister. We're not children living at home anymore. We are an empire."

"That is stronger when there are many of us."

"I agree with the many, and the less family I have, the more my children inherit."

The challenge was clear.

"You might be ahead when it comes to heirs, but my husband is lusty. I'm sure we'll soon catch up."

Damon coughed. Choked even. "Um," he said in a gasp, "while this family reunion is awesome, perhaps we should get going. Need I remind you, princess, we're only docking for a short time."

"How adorably delusional." Lunilla's hips swayed as she crossed the room and chose a floating, silver-covered settee to perch on. "No one comes to La'zuun for a short visit. It's a pleasure world. Meant to relax the mind. Engage the body."

"I can do those things on board the ship," Damon replied.

Maybe not the relax-the-mind part, but I can see my body being engaged. However, siding with Damon right now wouldn't go over well with her sister. Luni didn't like being ignored.

Michi placed a hand on his arm. "Surely, husband, a few more moments with my sister are allowed. We've just arrived." Michi shot him a look, but he didn't seem to get it. He thought she had a choice with this visit.

She didn't. Lunilla ordered. People, especially little sisters, obeyed.

"Maybe a few minutes," he grudgingly acquiesced.

"Sit." Lunilla pointed to other floating divans.

Michi chose the one closest to the door and accepted a drink from the hoverwaiter. She pretended to sip on it before asking, "How did you know I was on the planet?"

"I keep close tabs on my siblings." Spoken with a toothy grin that appeared too hungry.

"Are the children here?" She'd not seen her nephews in a long time.

"No. This is a vacation. No progeny allowed."

In other words, a lot like home where the children had their own separate wing along with a troop of nannies to care for them.

"It's a lovely place you're in."

"It's adequate." Her sister's nose wrinkled. "I would have preferred something grander, but some emperor and his entourage reserved the palace."

"How awful," was Damon's dry reply.

"Indeed. Almost as awful as my sister accidentally wedding a first mate. How did that happen?"

"Because it seemed a better choice than wedding the Kanishqui commander." Actually, the more time passed, the more she could see advantages in her choice of husband.

"Why does it matter how it happened?" Damon grumbled.

"It matters because I am curious as to how you came to find my sister. Especially if she was being held prisoner," Lunilla stated. "It seems rather fortuitous that you happened along."

"We didn't just happen along. Someone hired us to save her." Again, her husband jumped in with the truth, completely oblivious to her sister's machinations.

What is she doing? Because she knew Luni. If she'd brought Michonne to her, then there was a reason.

"Someone hired you to save her?" Lunilla sounded surprised. "Who would do that?"

Michi knew. "Papa, of course. He wanted his little girl saved." She batted her lashes. "You know how he dotes on me."

Lunilla gnashed her teeth. "He dotes on us all."

"Thank goodness he loves me so much he sent Damon to save me."

"You weren't in danger of dying."

"I might have been safe from death, but it was the other parts that worried me. We can't all be as lucky as you, dear sister, and marry a demi-god." Lunilla had wed into the most prestigious family in the universe. The son of the goddess Karma herself. There were a few entities that claimed deity status. Given their seeming immortality and inexplicable powers, no one dared to gainsay them. What was interesting was the fact their progeny didn't inherit the same attributes.

Lunilla never let them forget her children were one-quarter gods. She smiled fondly. "I am blessed to have my dear Herc and darling babies, Ares and Hermes. And now that you're married, you, too, can have children." She cast a glance first on Michonne then Damon. "I'm sure the geneticists can smooth out any problems."

The snub crested past subtle into insulting. It brought out the best in Michi. "Even they can only do so much with some flaws." She raised a hand to the tip of her nose and rubbed it.

Her sister—who'd had surgery to correct hers, and whose sons would need it, too—flushed. "You should have married the Kanishqui commander. I always wanted some freaks for nieces."

"Aren't you lucky. I'll have beautiful human ones instead."

"If they live. Children can be so fragile." Her sister's smile held the warmth of a dry, minus four-hundred-degree day on the icy plains. She was much more dangerous, too. Especially since she'd dropped the veneer of civility.

Michi stood. "This has been a lovely visit, but I really should depart now with my husband. Need to get started on those children." She offered her own insincere grin. "Kind of like apples, they are just so much better when they're made naturally." The dig wasn't lost. Her sister valued her body too much to let it undergo the vagaries of birth and was much too in control to allow another female to carry her genes. She relied on the more modern electronic womb. Yet, there were those that claimed those born of machine weren't the same. They were often drawn to the tech.

"You can't leave yet. We have much to catch up on. Come and let us go to the garden. We'll leave your husband here. Herc will be along shortly to entertain him."

Damon did nothing when the guards, silent until now, drew close, flanking him.

"So kind of you to invite us, but we're leaving. My husband needs to ensure the ship is ready for departure." She made to move toward Damon, only to have her sister clamp onto her arm.

"I said we weren't done, *sister*. This would have been much simpler if you'd married the Kanishqui commander as planned. Do you know how much you cost me?"

"Cost you?" The realization dawned as she stared at her sister. "That's how the Kanishqui force got through our defenses so easily. I knew Papa didn't want me to marry it."

"Papa wouldn't have cared once it was done. And we both know how he feels about Kaniman hybrids."

It wasn't the fact that the children were butt ugly with tentacles and an inability to speak in human or Kanishqui. Papa had no use for them because they were sterile. Kanishqui and humans could mate, with help, but their progeny would never reproduce. Which meant... "You were trying to ensure when I died you got a bigger share." Because sterile family members couldn't inherit.

"Not me. My heirs. My sons." Said with a haughtily lifted chin.

"I'll see you those sons and throw in some daughters." She'd birth an army if she had to. While daughters were preferred by the Dkar to expand the family and make alliances, in most cultures, it was the males who inherited instead.

"Don't start a war with me, little sister. We might not be allowed to directly kill each other"—or they were automatically out of the will—"but I can make things difficult."

Michi tilted her chin. "So can I. Husband, I'd like to go back to the ship now. That is, if you think you can get us there."

"Did you have to say it that way?" he groaned.

She tossed him a look, and her lips twisted a little as she said, "Is this your way of saying you couldn't possibly handle these two rather humanoid guards and that you're going to let my sister have her wicked way?"

His lips pulled down. "I expect you to explain this to the captain. Tell him it wasn't my fault." Uttered a moment before Damon moved. His arm lashed out and hit the first guard in the chest, causing him to cough and reel. He whirled and kicked at the other guard, who started to raise his weapon, only Damon snared it. He pulled it free, flipped it, and fired.

The guard dropped. Damon pivoted and shot again, the other guard's weapon discharging harmlessly into the ceiling as he fell.

"Gua—" Her sister opened her mouth, and Michi was on her, slapping a hand over it. Lunilla bit her, and Michi yelped.

"Get off me," her sister snapped.

"Call off your guards," Michi retorted, grappling with Lunilla.

"Things were much better before you came around."

"You can leave anytime you like," she offered.

"I hope you die a quick death and are forgotten forever."

"What an awful thing to say. And here I wasn't going to wish you lost all your wealth and were forced to live on a colony planet, begging on the streets, scrounging in the garbage for food."

An inarticulate cry burst from Lunilla. She shoved Michi away from her, and Michi lost her balance, tripping over the inert body of a guard. Her sister took that moment to flee.

A grunt had her whirling to see her husband was a little busy. Apparently, the meeting was watched, and when trouble was spotted, more soldiers had poured into the room—and they all wanted her husband.

He tussled with the guards, boldly punching, even kneeing them. His skill, while impressive, wasn't a match for the numbers against him.

And the guns.

Weapons fired, and yet somehow Damon remained unaffected. The bright spots hit him, and his body shimmered as if absorbing it.

A body shield. She'd never even suspected. Nice, and for one of that quality, pricey. He fired in return, dropping the soldiers, creating a heaping pile of bodies.

"Are they dead?" she asked. Not that it mattered. This kind of attack wouldn't go unnoticed.

"Sleeping. I had my gun set to stun. And I'd be less worried about them than your psycho sister. If that's a sample of your family, then I'm really getting worried about meeting your daddy."

"He's actually not as a bad as my grandmother," she muttered. Nana had been known to kill family members that got on her bad side. "We should leave. Lunilla isn't the type to accept losing."

"Did I hear her right?" he asked, lacing his fingers through hers and tugging her through the kitchen area and then out a door into an alley. "Did your sister try and arrange a marriage between you and the octopus?"

"Yes." A brilliant move and one she should have expected. She'd known of her sister's ruthlessness. She'd just never been subjected to it as the youngest.

Until now. Would this mean she needed to expect her other sisters to make attempts, too? Lunilla's admission at least answered the question of how the security of her home was breached and her kidnapping achieved so easily. She'd have to better guard herself in the future.

"Are you worth that much?"

"Haven't you checked?"

He shot her a glance. "Yes, but astronomical isn't really a number."

"It's enough to make all kinds of people a little stupid."

"A little? Again, your sister tried to marry you off to seafood."

"Because she's not allowed to have me killed." Entire family lines had disappeared before the Dkar religion introduced a codicil that banned direct acts of deadly violence against family members.

"Does this spat mean I won't have to endure family dinners?"

"There will be dinners," she said, dropping her voice to an ominous level as he took her through a long alley lined with concrete ditches.

"And lots of kids, apparently. You want quite a few by the sounds of it," he noted, changing track. He paused at the corner of the alley and peered out cautiously.

"A half-dozen, maybe more, to ensure some survive to their adult years and can take over the family wealth." While the Dkar did not condone, and punished, assassination attempts, it still happened.

"That's pretty cutthroat."

"Welcome to my culture."

"Are there any more surprises I should know about?"

She didn't reply. One didn't just talk about it. Only those indoctrinated could know all the secrets.

"Is your father really going to kill me?"

"Not if I can help it."

He paused at the corner of another alley to face her. "Not reassuring, princess."

"Neither is this rescue so far. Do you even know where you're going?"

"Nope. I figure at one point we can pop out and ask directions to the ship."

The ship, which she kind of wish she'd never left. But what could she do when she received the missive? After her sister was done bragging about yet another heir, she added a postscript.

Accidents are so common in the marketplace. Hope your new husband doesn't have one. L.

She knew better than to meet her sister alone. Yet how could Michi stay onboard with that threat hanging over him? Not that she would tell him that was why she left. Admit she cared what happened to him? He'd never believe it.

Or would he? He had, after all, come to her rescue.

She leaned up on tiptoe and kissed him. A quick embrace that had him muttering, "What was that for?"

"For being my husband."

"Save that for later. Let's get out of here."

He finally found an alley he liked, or at least an exit that met his approval, because he slid open a door and tugged her through the back into an active part of La'zuun. The slave market.

Being sheltered didn't mean Michi didn't grasp what she saw. Framed in windows were people. Mostly humanoid, female, and pretty. Two breasts, three, a handful. Big lips. Long hair. Wide hips. As young as the laws allowed. And old, for those with that fetish.

To his credit, Damon didn't peek at the naked flesh

on display. He tucked her close to his side and maneuvered them past those gawking, pointing, and, in many cases, purchasing. Slavery was a fact of life in the universe. Some of them captives of fate, others volunteering to earn money to pay off debt or to help family.

Suddenly, he veered them in the other direction. She laughed. "Did you just find your bearings?"

"I think we might have some company."

"Who? My sister?"

"Try ex-fiancé."

"He found us? I thought we lost him." She tried to glance over her shoulder, but their quick pace and the crowd made it hard to see anything.

"We should have lost him. The chances of us both being here at the same time are..."

He didn't have to say it because she already knew it was astronomical, which could mean only one thing. "Someone let him know we were coming here." Their pace quickened.

"Except we didn't even know we were coming until the captain told us."

"The captain knew."

"Jameson wouldn't rat you out. More likely our route was being beamed by a mole, and they shadowed us until they could attack."

"What can he possibly hope to gain? We're wed. He can't change that."

"He could kill me and make you a widow."

Over her dead body. "Making me a widow doesn't reset the mark. The mark requires a period of mourning before becoming active again in order to prevent such a scenario."

"Well, perhaps someone should explain that to him." They veered abruptly again, this time darting into a shop offering oils. The warmth of the place hit her along with a flowery fragrance. Within the shop, the chaotic movement and sound of the marketplace vanished for the more serene space of the oil store with its small bubbling pots.

"Where are we supposed to hide?" she asked, looking around.

"Not hiding, looking for a rear entrance. Where do you bring in the goods? The back door?" he asked the shopkeeper, a vermillion slug sitting in a corner smoking a pipe.

"Blurg. Da blurg. Blurg."

"For fuck's sake. Fine. I'll buy this shit, whatever it is." He pointed to a bubbling blue oil. The vendor extended a device, his slug-like body projecting a limb that kept going and going to reach Damon.

Damon slapped his hand on it, transferring the credits. "Now, where's that back door?"

In moments, they were stepping into the alley, and just in time.

Rushing water over rocks. *Where did they go?*

They gained precious minutes as the shopkeeper made the Kanishqui go through the same charade.

"Why are we running?" she asked, attempting to keep pace with her long-legged husband. "He can't attack us here. There are rules."

"Yup. And there's also looking the other way and bribery."

"You seem very experienced in this."

He paused by another door, unmarked, and yet something about it drew him because he rapped on it.

"I've had to escape a few places in my time."

The door opened, and a face peered out. The hawkishly long nose warted at the tip, the hair a frizzy black. "Whatcha want?"

"I need to get back to my ship."

A bleary eye squinted. "It will cost you."

"When doesn't it?" Damon grumbled, slapping his hand against the credit reader.

"I'll repay the expenses," Michi offered.

He shot her a glare. "Don't you dare. You're my wife. My responsibility."

The witch, whom Michi recognized by the crest burnt into her cheek—a switch in a circle—let them into her shop. The door slid shut, and the smell of something bubbling on a fire tickled her nose.

"Give me a moment to fetch the ingredients." The witch waddled to a wall, the shelves a rare wood, the bottles on it labeled by hand and stoppered. The witch truly embraced her roots and made sure her business reflected it.

She pulled down three flasks, poured a measure from each into a bowl, then approached them. "Don't move," she admonished as she took a feathery whisk and dipped it into the fluid. Then she shook it at them. The droplets hit Michi's skin, and she made a face.

"What's she doing?" she asked.

"Shhh." The witch flung more juice at her. It hit her flesh and tingled. Then burned. A moment later, she was on her knees, writhing, mouth open wide on a scream that wouldn't escape. When it was done, she was curled in a ball.

A stranger crouched beside her. "You all right there, princess?" The words sounded like Damon and yet...

"Who are you?"

He laughed and held out his hand. "Your husband for the next hour. Come on. We need to move before the spell wears off."

A spell, as in magic. Or, as the witches claimed in their marketing, a temporary suspension of belief and science.

A glimpse in a mirror showed her looking like... "A man? You made me a man?" she squeaked. Just proving her point that the male crew had some kind of affliction because, sure enough, she looked like an ensign, uniform and all.

"We'll stand out less when we take the shortcut."

"There's a shortcut?"

Apparently, there was an aerial tram back to the space launch, closely watched by soldiers. She tucked close to Damon. "Are you sure they can't tell it's us?"

"Keep talking and we'll find out."

She clamped her lips shut.

The tram arrived, and the doors opened. The

soldiers watched everyone getting on. Especially the women.

Looking for me?

She sat down, and a chair suctioned her butt into it. She began to relax as the strange body Damon wore sat across from her. He tapped his fingers on the armrest. The tram took its time leaving the station.

"What are they waiting for?"

They waited for more soldiers to enter the train and slowly walk the aisle while the passengers chatted. She didn't feel like chattering, but knew it would look odd if she didn't.

"What did you buy in the marketplace?" she asked, startled by the distinctly male voice that emerged from her lips.

"Present for the wife."

Wife? *That's me!* "Oh. What did you get?"

Before he could reply, the soldiers reached them. A fellow in a black facemask, only his dark eyes showing, perused her. "Name and ship."

She had only a second to think. "Lieutenant Goweranski. The *Gypsy Moth*."

"Proof please." They held out a device, a scanner of the type she'd seen Damon using to pay for products. She knew what would happen if she put her hand on it. The disguise would fail. She shot a panicked look at Damon, only to see him rising from his seat. "Fucking pigs," he yelled before darting out the door.

She almost joined him even as she realized he acted

to draw the guards away. There was shouting outside the tram doors, and she half rose to see him being tackled to the ground, the guards having gotten wind of the fact that his shield protected him from attack.

The door swished suddenly shut, and the tram moved, leaving him behind. She felt a moment's panic.

I have to go back. To do what? She didn't have the skills to save him. But she knew someone who did.

The moment the tram arrived at the spaceport, she spilled out and went running. The *Gypsy Moth* loomed on the tarmac, a hulking ghost ship compared to the smaller, sleeker vessels, but an ally. She sprinted past the crew returning to it, weaving around them until she reached the ship. She slapped a hand against the first communication console she found, wishing her religion didn't ban the use of embedded technology. Times like these, she could have used a communication device. "Ship, give me the captain."

"The captain is busy at this time. Please leave a message."

"This is important."

"Message received."

She blinked at the wall. "No, that wasn't my message. I need his help. Now. They took Damon."

"All personnel, please board the vessel and prepare for departure," the computer announced, the volume of it loud enough to add haste to the stragglers still entering.

She stood to the side, frustrated. *I can't leave him here.*

Her sister might not kill him because, after all, a living yet absent husband wasn't impregnating her, but she wasn't sure about the Kanishqui commander.

A light framing the door began to flash. A final warning to get on the ship.

Only Michi still remained outside. She took a deep breath. She was probably making a colossal mistake, and yet she remained on the tarmac. Walked away from the ship actually.

Someone had to save Damon. While she lacked any kind of skill to do so, she was wagering on one important thing.

Given who her daddy was, the captain wouldn't leave without her. Which was why she lifted her head high when the soldiers surrounded her and Michi demanded, quite imperially, "Take me to my husband."

CHAPTER 11

THE ROOM they marched Damon to didn't contain much. A chain dangling from the ceiling. A stain on the floor.

This is gonna hurt.

Yet, what else could he do? He knew those soldiers were looking for a woman. His woman.

He'd sacrificed himself to save her, but that didn't mean he was going to accept the torture easily. And yes, he assumed torture because they hadn't killed him the moment they managed to deactivate his body shield.

Despite his manacled hands, Damon caused some trouble—head butting a guard, lashing out with his feet —but they overcame him by sheer number, tackling him to the floor then dragging him upright to chain him.

He dangled, arms pulled taut, his toes barely scraping the floor. It put him in a rather precarious predicament when Fizz, that tentacled bastard, made an appearance. Given he was planet-side, the giant octopus male wore a hoverharness, allowing his body to float above the ground.

He also held a whip.

Gushing sewage through a grate. *Mangy human. How dare you think to steal what was promised me?*

Since cockiness couldn't make things much worse, Damon retorted, "Not my fault she chose the better man."

Slap. The slimy tentacle whipped across his face, leaving a trail of slime behind.

You stole her.

"She chose me. We're married, slimeball. Get over it. Find yourself a new woman."

It's not over. And she won't be married to you for long. Fizz gestured, and someone approached, a short roach-like creature, his orange carapace bright, his many eyes unblinking. He held some kind of device.

"Open your mouth." The stilted words were robotic sounding as the roach thing spoke.

"The orphanage taught me not to listen to strangers."

"I am Doctor Pinceaux. Open."

"Why?"

"The word is you want a divorce. We're here to grant it."

A divorce?

Hurry up. Fizz jiggled with impatience.

"This is a delicate procedure," the doctor advised.

"Hold him still. And open his mouth." The guards approached, and Damon twisted in his chains, only to freeze as a commotion outside the room drew everyone's attention.

The door slid open, and Fizz burbled, *What is it? Why do you disturb me?*

Someone was thrust into the space, and Damon could have groaned when he saw Michonne suddenly appear.

The Kanishqui commander jiggled with giddiness, a swirling soup of sloshing excitement. *Excellent. This will make things even easier.*

Easier to do what? Damon didn't think he'd like the answer.

"I thought you escaped?" he hissed as Michonne flew to his side and surveyed him, her lower lip caught between her teeth.

"I did. But the ship was going to leave without you."

"And you should have gone with it. Why the hell didn't you go?"

She shrugged. "You're my husband."

Not for long.

The doctor approached. "Hold him still while I remove the mark."

"Remove?" Michonne whirled. "You can't remove it. It will kill him."

"An unfortunate side effect."

Fear not, you won't be widowed long. The doctor

has found a way to transfer the mark without a reset or waiting period.

"You can't do that." Michonne tried to shield Damon with her body, but it took only a single Kanishqui guard to hold her out of the way.

The approaching roach raised his device, and no matter how Damon squirmed, he couldn't escape the guards holding his mouth open.

Just as the whirring device got close, the door blasted open. He blinked at the dust and then grinned as the chain overhead suddenly let loose.

He immediately brought his hands forward, still tethered, and clubbed the nearest guard. Who dropped his weapon.

"Grab it," Damon shouted to Michonne, who stared wide-eyed at the chaos.

Captain Jameson had arrived, wielding a huge gun —the kind that left big holes—and he was shooting anything that moved. Which worked great on the guards, but Fizz wasn't going down.

"Fucker stole my body shield." What Fizz didn't know was it had a limited battery life.

Damon held up his tethered hands and shouted, "Twelve o'clock."

It was Ivan, with a wide grin, who raised a gun and fired. Damon's hands split apart, still wearing bracelets, but at least now he could join the fight.

Michonne had grabbed a weapon and backed herself against the wall. Probably the best spot for her since more bodies floated into the room, the Kanishqui crew coming to help their commander.

Damon dove at a waving tentacle and wrestled away a gun. He joined the captain, Ivan, and the ensigns who were laying down weapon fire.

But everyone froze when they heard the big splash.

*Stop or I kill the heiress.

Fizz had managed to capture Michonne and held her against him. She looked more pissed than scared. However, Damon was scared enough for the two of them given Fizz held a knife to her throat.

"He won't kill me," she stated. "He wants my fortune."

Gurgling, laughing brook. *If I can't have your fortune, then I will settle for a boon from your sibling.

"Lunilla won't reward you for killing me."

*Your sister harbors great hatred for you.

Speaking of whom, Lunilla strode into the room and replied, "I hate her yes, but I would never reward anyone for killing my baby sister. And how dare you even assume that." Lunilla raised her gun. Fizz managed to have his tentacles look smug, and then he was sushi as her shot blew off the top of his head.

The battery on his shield had run out.

And so had their invitation to the planet.

CHAPTER 12

MICHONNE and the crew of the *Gypsy Moth* weren't the only ones asked to depart the planet. Lunilla and her entourage had to leave, too. But at least she fared better than the Kanishqui. For their violent actions against La'zuun guests, they were rounded up and taken prisoner. Some whispered they would make a fine stew.

Gag.

Michonne did manage a hug with her sister before they were taken to their respective ships. She whispered, "Thanks for coming to my aid."

"I hope you're barren," was her sister's reply.

Aboard the ship, there was some chaos as they prepared to depart. With nothing to do, she went to her room while Damon went to give his report to the captain.

She flopped onto the bed. Alive and kind of amazed. When she'd made the split-second decision to save Damon, she'd not thought it through very well. She'd acted. Acted to save the man who consumed her thoughts. When she'd seen him, suspended and bloody, she'd been so worried. What if her plan failed? What if he died?

She didn't want him to die. *Because I care about him.*

They'd known each other only a short time, and yet he'd come to mean something to her. He was her husband, and today, by sacrificing himself, he'd shown himself also to be her protector.

And soon, her lover.

When the door finally opened, she was ready.

"Husband." She greeted him with a soft smile and not a stitch of clothing. His eyes widened. His wounds had been tended and his skin cleaned. However, that didn't stop her from taking him by the hand and leading him into the bathing chamber.

He studied her as she stripped him, acting as his servant, revealing all that lovely taut flesh.

"Why did you come back?"

"I thought I already answered this," she said, disposing of his clothes and trying to keep her gaze averted from his thickening cock.

"You did, but I don't understand. You could have escaped. Avoided that mess."

"That would have involved leaving you to die."

"And?" He held a question in his eyes.

She placed her hands on his chest, feeling the heat

of him through her palms. "I don't want you to die. *Husband.*" She said the word low, and he growled.

"Marriage to you is dangerous."

"It is."

"You're dangerous."

The cleansing air jets turned on as she tilted her head. "How am I dangerous?"

His hands spanned her waist and drew her into the molten heat of his body. "Because you make me want things."

"Like?" she whispered.

He didn't reply, rather instead crushed his mouth to hers, instantly igniting the passion that always simmered between them.

She opened her mouth that their tongues might dance. The heat of their breath mingled. Their skin touched, awakening a tingling from head to toe, and especially in between. She found herself shoved against the smooth wall of the shower unit, her butt pressed right against the spot one of the lights tried to beam and clean. It heated her skin, but she didn't care as he braced himself against her, one hand on the wall, the other reaching to cup a breast. She arched at the contact, pushing the curve of her breast further into his palm.

He brushed his thumb over it and murmured against her lips, "I can't believe I'm here with you."

The reminder of how close they'd come to losing each other brought on a fierce need. She grabbed his head and kissed him hard, their teeth banging, and still she couldn't get enough of him.

He tore his mouth from hers, and she mewled in protest, only to sigh as he ducked his head that he might brush his lips across the tip of her breast. Electrifying. Her whole body quivered. Then went rigid as he sucked on the erect nipple.

"Yes," she gasped, only to cry out as he bit down on the tip. He swirled his tongue around the peak before sucking at it again, tugging at her flesh.

She closed her eyes, losing herself in the enjoyment. Feeling every suck and nibble not only on her breasts but between her legs, too.

The play went two ways. As he touched her, so did she touch him, her hands stroking over his broad shoulders, raking her nails on his skin.

She stroked lower, running her fingers down his ribcage to his buttocks. She dug her fingers into that taut flesh, and he grunted. But he didn't stop playing. Damon alternated between tugging on her taut nipples with his lips and licking them. When he bit down, her whole body jerked.

She parted her legs for the insistent thrust of his thigh and then rode it, rubbing her mound against him, the hard muscle providing a friction for her throbbing sex.

When he replaced that thigh with his cock, she grabbed it, delighted to have something harder to play with. She used it to rub her clitoris, the fat head of his shaft just right for stimulating her.

He groaned. "If you don't stop..."

He'd lose control? What a lovely thing to say.

Arousal coursed through her body. She was more than ready for him, and yet he seemed intent on teasing.

And pleasing.

He dropped to his knees, spread her thighs, and palmed her buttocks, pulling her forward against his mouth. She groaned at the first lick.

Moaned at the second.

He lashed her with his tongue, back and forth, drawing panted cries. He stabbed into her, licking at her honey before teasing her button again.

Her head thrashed as she moaned. "Yes. Yes." He kept licking and brought things to a new level by thrusting two fingers into her. "Damon!" She said his name as a small climax hit, a ripple that clenched his fingers tight.

Only then did he finally stand, the throbbing tip of his cock poking at her. She wrapped her arms around his shoulders as he lifted her, aligning her with his body, plunging his shaft into her welcoming sheath.

He might have growled, "Mine." She knew she did. The thrust rammed him right through her maidenhead, stretched her, and claimed in a way her mark never did. Brought her more pleasure than she could have imagined.

For a moment, she could have sworn time slowed, and within that pocket only she and Damon existed. Two souls combining into one.

Then the climax hit. And by climax, she meant she lost her mind. She certainly keened and cried out as her body shuddered with the ecstasy of it. She thought she heard him shout as he spurted hotly into her body.

In that moment, she knew this was the only man for her. Her husband. She had never felt anything more right.

And when it was done, he caught her in his arms and buried his face in her arm. Just held her. Didn't ruin it with words. Didn't say anything at all. But when they were snuggled in bed, naked, their bodies intertwined, she happily murmured, "Thank you."

His reply? "Always."

Their next session proved just an intense. As did the one after. They indulged several times that night. Yet she awoke refreshed and smiling to find him watching her.

"Good morning, wife."

"Is it morning already?" She stretched and noted how his gaze watched, and smoldered. "I'm surprised you're still here. Shouldn't you be off exercising with your friends?"

"I took the day off to relax."

By relax he meant spend it with her. In bed. It was heavenly. The days following that pure bliss. It was also a time of discovery.

As he got called on various tasks, sometimes dragging her along, she began to understand what he did on the ship. Pretty much anything the captain couldn't.

Which kept Damon busy. But not so busy that he ignored her when his workday was done.

They fell into a routine, one of discovery, play, and work.

It was perfect, which meant it couldn't last.

She was learning how to fire a weapon in the holodeck to avoid being so useless in the next fight when she was paged by her husband.

"Michi, can you come to the bridge?"

Her husband's request emerged from the wrist transmitter he'd gotten her. This wasn't the first time he'd asked her to meet him there. Anytime the *Moth* came across an interesting galactic phenomenon, he wanted to show her. They shared everything like a real couple should.

With a smile on her lips, she almost skipped to see him. She entered the bridge and opened her mouth to say hello, only to freeze. She blinked, certain it was a mirage, but the man didn't disappear.

"Papa? How did you get here?"

Her father, dressed in a dark blue uniform, adorned with silver weave that glistened, was a big man in his own right, tall and strong, yet showing signs of age in the lines of his face and the gray of his hair—that he refused to dye—turned. "Daughter. I've come to bring you home."

"I have a home. Here on this ship."

Papa's lips flattened. "You are not staying on the *Gypsy Moth*."

"I'll have to discuss it with Damon." A man who stood ramrod still and silent, but his eyes...they blazed.

"It's not up to him." Her father folded his arms over his chest.

"He's my husband."

"Not for long."

When her father moved toward Damon, she flung herself between them. "Don't you dare kill him."

"I wasn't planning to. The man did the family a service when he rescued you from that slimy Kanishqui. But you're worth more than a mere first mate. Which is why I got dispensation to dissolve the wedding."

"What?" Her eyes widened. "I thought it wasn't possible."

"Only under special circumstances. Given you married to avoid an alliance with someone you deemed unsuitable, and the first mate's recorded reluctance, I was given an annulment protocol."

"What's that mean?" Damon asked.

"It means," Father said, turning his gaze on Damon, "that you will be compensated for your service to the family and free to continue with your life."

"What if I don't want a divorce?" she asked.

The dark gaze of her father turned back to Michi. "Your wants aren't the question here. Family honor and alliances are. The good news is you won't need to wait a mourning period, and I've lined up a few suitable suitors. I think it's past time we settled this situation."

"You can't just decide that for us," Damon argued.

"It's already done. The signal for the annulment was sent the moment you entered the room. The bond is being severed as we speak."

Damon coughed. Then coughed again, raising his hand and then lowering it to show a spot of liquid metal. Her mark.

Father signaled to one of his people, and a woman scooped the puddle into a box. "It is done."

"But..." Her arms were grabbed, with Damon looking on, his expression grim. "Aren't you going to do something?"

"It's probably for the best, princess."

Best for who? She wanted to scream, *I love you.* But did he feel the same way? Wouldn't he fight for her if he truly wanted her?

She cast one last look over her shoulder. A longing one, and for a moment, he met her gaze, anguish in it, quickly covered by a placid mask.

He wouldn't stop her father from taking her away.

Did nothing as she was boarded onto her father's luxury cruiser. Did not even try to contact her as they left that galaxy, heading for home.

Her meager pile of things was waiting for her in the stateroom assigned. Including a tiny box.

A gift? She was tempted to toss it. Why keep a gift from a man who didn't love her? And why hadn't he given it to her before? What was inside?

Curiosity won. She flipped open the lid and sobbed when she saw the ring nestled within.

CHAPTER 13

THE BETRAYAL on Michi's face haunted Damon. He couldn't help reliving it over and over as she was taken away from him.

It should have been a happy moment. They'd not wanted to be wed. Never wanted a forever together. Yet, something had happened to them. A bond had formed. He'd initially blamed it on the mark. Blamed it for how he felt.

However, he was no longer legally bound to Michonne. He was a free and single man. Then why the hell did he miss her so much? Why did he keep wishing he'd done something different? Done something, period.

What could he have done, though? Start a war with her father?

I could have said something about how I felt. Except he didn't truly understand his emotions until she left.

I love her. Loved her and lost her. And soon, if her father had his way, she'd be married off to someone suitable and forget all about him.

With that worry in mind, he scoured the gossip channels. And when those didn't feed his need to see her, he dug deeper. Hired—also known as bribing—someone in her father's household to send him news.

What he received was a picture. A picture of Michi dressed in a splendid gown, her hair intricately woven atop her head, her expression hinting of sadness, and on her finger, her ring finger...

"Holy fuck, she's wearing it." The ring he'd had stowed in her things as they were packed. A ring he held on to and forgot until he had to pack her things and send them to her father's ship.

Now, it could be she wore it just because she thought it pretty. However, Damon took it as a sign. A sign he wasn't about to ignore.

Which was why he found himself in the captain's quarters, handing in his resignation.

Jameson peered at him over the holomessage. "You're quitting? To do what?"

"I'd rather not say anything that might compromise you, sir."

"This is about the woman."

"My wife."

"Not according to her father."

"It's not his decision."

"What makes you think she wants you? Has she called?"

Damon shook his head.

"Then why would you ditch your position and go running after her?"

"Why haven't you divorced and remarried?" he countered.

Jameson's expression turned hard. "You do realize you're choosing a difficult path if you go after her."

"I love her, sir."

The captain slashed his finger over the holomessage, shredding it. "In that case, I refuse your resignation and am not granting you leave to depart this ship."

"Sir, you—"

Jameson wasn't done. "Ship, advise our head engineer we need to streak ASAP. My first mate has a woman he needs to rescue."

"Sir?" Damon couldn't help sounding confused. "I don't understand. He's your friend."

"So are you, Damon. If you're willing to ditch your career and risk your life, then who I am to stand in your way? And I wouldn't be a good friend if I didn't offer to help."

"How will we get her? Her home is closely guarded. They won't just let us waltz in and take her."

The captain aimed his next statement at the ceiling. "Patch me through to Einstein. Please advise her the captain requires her aid with something."

"What do you want?" the ornery tech specialist barked, her voice coming through the embedded speakers.

"The first mate needs to bypass an impenetrable security system, kidnap a woman, and escape."

"Why don't I kill him now and save us the trouble?" was Einstein's smart-ass reply.

"Are you saying you can't do it?" the captain teased, and Damon couldn't help but smirk as their tech guru was challenged.

"You're an asshole," she grumbled. "I'll get him in and out, but I want that new cloaking technology the Bezonians have been hoarding."

"Deal."

And that easily, Damon found himself being teleported to a planet, his cells melted down and reconfigured—resulting in him patting himself down to ensure he was all there—and bypassing the various levels of security.

But dammit, at least he wasn't on board the ship moping.

Now he only hoped he'd read things right and Michonne would be happy to see him.

CHAPTER 14

Pacing in her room, Michonne kept an eye on the time. She couldn't rush, or everything would fall apart. Papa had done his best to cut her off from the outside world, claiming she needed to recover from her ordeal.

Did he suspect what she planned? Possibly, given she'd slid on the ring Damon had given her the moment she saw it nestled in the fabric of the box. She understood what the piece of jewelry meant. He'd bought it for her. A symbol that he had accepted and chosen her as his mate.

Papa thought he could annul her marriage and that she would just start over. However, no one could erase her feelings for Damon, and now that she knew he'd planned to try and make it work, she wasn't about to settle for anyone else. No matter what Papa wanted.

What about what I want? She used to think she wanted the power of a strong alliance. To multiply her great net worth. To marry someone that would make her father proud. Seeing her sister, though— the shallowness of her life—Michi realized she wanted more.

Which was why, when the three moons rose in the sky and crossed paths in a rare triple eclipse, she drew on her cloak and hid within its hood as she exited her room. The electronics that monitored the mansion would be rendered almost useless as the lunar interference from the eclipses frazzled the signals. Long enough that she made it out of her room and into the hall where she had to rely on the luminescent carpet runner to guide her steps.

What she didn't expect was for hands to grip her.

Not another attempted kidnapping. She thrashed. "Unhand me!" Panic and annoyance made her kick and hit.

An exclaimed, "Ouch," drew a gasp from her.

"Damon?" she queried.

"Hey, princess."

Her heart fluttered. "What are you doing here?"

"A husband's place is with his wife."

The words had her throwing her arms around his neck and clasping him tight. "You came for me."

"Of course I did. We're married."

"Not according to my father or the law."

"Fuck the law. I love you, and we belong together."

At his declaration, she lifted on tiptoe to mash her mouth against his and murmur, "I love you, too."

And the moment might have gotten friskier had the captain not grumbled, "Can you save it for later? We don't have much time before the systems come back online and someone notices we've penetrated the building."

"Let's go, princess." He laced his fingers in hers, and they ran down the hall, following the shadowy shape of the captain, skirting the occasional snoring lumps on the floor. Damon had mounted a full-on rescue.

He came for me. He loves me. The giddiness of it all made her smile even as anxiety gripped her.

Papa wouldn't like this turn of events, but he'd have to understand this was her life.

A life he guarded too closely.

Bright lights suddenly illuminated the main floor where the stairs ended.

She shielded her gaze with a hand as Papa barked, "And just where do you think you're going?"

Damon chose to reply. "She's coming with me."

Father sneered. "Figures you'd return. The lure of her wealth was too much, I guess."

Damon held himself tall. "Fuck her money. You can keep it. I have enough for us to live decently on."

"You expect her to become the wife of a common space farer?" Papa said with clear disdain.

"I don't care about his position," she said, stepping forward. "I love him. He makes me happy."

"Happiness can be fleeting."

"Or last a lifetime." She stood tall. Taller than she'd ever stood, especially against her father. "My life. My choice."

"And if I said it's not up to you? That I will choose?" Papa barked.

"Then I will defy you every chance I get. Marry me to someone and I will make myself a widow."

To her surprise, her father smiled. "Then I give you my blessing."

She blinked. "What?" Seriously, because she thought she'd heard...

"I said you have my blessing. I was wondering how long it would take him to make an attempt. I knew you were plotting."

She blinked. "Hold on. You knew we wanted to be together?"

"From the moment you placed your mark on him."

"But how?" When she didn't even know herself. "And if you knew, why divorce us?"

"Because you both needed the realization that you belonged together. To fight for it."

"You never did this to my sisters."

"Your sisters only ever had one goal in mind—more power and wealth. But you waited. And kept waiting. I realized you weren't like them. That you had a different goal in mind."

"And you're not angry?"

Papa shrugged. "Angry that you're like me? Your mother also had a father who tried to deny our affection for each other."

"I thought my grandpapa was dead."

"He is. I killed him when he wouldn't back down

and let me have your mother. But I am hoping we can avoid that scenario in this case."

"Oh, Papa." She flew to him and threw her arms around his neck.

He grumbled something gruff about silly female emotions. Then insisted they all go have a drink.

She didn't pay much attention to what was said beyond the fact that she could be with Damon.

He pulled her aside at one point and said, "Are you sure this is what you want?"

"More than anything I've ever wanted before." She then cupped his face and kissed him. Then kissed him again until her father barked, "Get a room."

If he insisted.

CHAPTER 15

Hand in hand with Michonne, Damon followed where she led. His head still spun from all that had happened. He'd expected to have to fight his way out. To possibly be imprisoned or even rejected. What he'd not expected was to find himself in a luxury suite, in a mansion beyond anything he'd ever seen, with the woman he loved.

Before he wasted any more time, he dropped to his knees, clasped her hand, and stared up at her lovely face flushed with excitement. Her eyes shone bright. The words he wanted to say, gushing romantic things, stuck in his throat. All he managed was, "Will you be my wife?"

"I never stopped."

He drew her hand to his lips and kissed the ring she wore. "In sickness and health, in riches or poor, until we are dust on a galactic wind, together forever."

"That's a much prettier speech than what I need," she said, dropping to her knees before him.

He smiled. And repeated the fateful words that started their love affair, finishing with a very sure, "I do."

When she kissed him, it stole his breath, and when she bit him, he welcomed it, welcomed her mark and her love.

Then he took her to bed.

Tossed her on it, actually, before tearing at his clothes. She still managed to denude herself first and beckoned him.

He fell on her, a hungry beast, a man too long without the touch of his woman.

He caressed all of her, his lips trailing a path over every inch of her body. His cock claiming her molten sex with firm thrusts that she welcomed with fingers digging into his back.

When they both came, it was more beautiful than anything in the galaxy. Worth living and dying for.

This was love.

EPILOGUE

BEING the first mate's wife, by design rather than accident the second time round, proved more exciting than expected. For one, she got to see places Papa had previously forbidden. Damon tried to forbid her too; however, aboard the *Gypsy Moth,* she discovered a freedom she'd never had at home. She even acquired a job. Guest Event Coordinator. The captain had noticed her event planning on board for the Nexus and corralled her into expanding that work for alien clients and dignitaries.

"Another party?" Damon groaned as he entered their quarters to find swatches of colorful fabrics all over.

"We're meeting with the Mor'omonan and his eighteen spouses. They're thinking of hiring the ship on their celestial tour."

"And that needs a party?" He held up something fluffy. "Whatever happened to a handshake in a bar?"

"That's for short-term deals. The real money is in the longer contracts. And the captain agrees. He's also talking about buying a second ship." An armored fighter to guard the *Moth,* given they'd be carrying very important people.

"I know about the other ship. He asked me to captain it."

"And?" she asked, knowing how he felt about being in command.

"I get to blow shit up. What do you think I said?"

She squealed and dove over the fabric cutouts to throw herself at him. "That's amazing." Her husband would be a captain.

And that was just the start. With a burgeoning life growing in her body, it was time to create a legacy they could pass on. A fleet of starships would make a nice start.

She had ideas for new uniforms. And...

"I can see your mind smoking with ideas."

"Then why don't you distract me," she teased.

So he did. He distracted her with kisses and made love to her amongst the stars.

CRANK EYED THE SECOND REACTOR, its feeble glow indicating they still had more to repair. Good thing they'd finally gotten a cargo that might actually work this time.

Bloody charlatans in the ports, promising one thing, delivering another. When that happened, Crank paid them a visit and reminded them why it wasn't a good idea to screw him over.

"Chief!" One of the ensigns yelled for him. "We've got a problem with that last crate we ordered from La'zuun."

Which contained silicia, an organic material that resembled a fluffy pile of leaves, purple ones with hair-like filaments that were valuable in the creation of holochips for a variety of items.

"What the hell is wrong now?" he muttered as he stomped over.

"There's something alive in the crate." The ensign indicated with a pointed finger. "Should we shoot it?"

Alive after weeks of being in space? Probably a rodent. Pesky buggers were hard to kill. "Don't do anything." Firing into the silicia would destroy them. Given their cost, and the need for them, they couldn't afford to lose even a single one. "Is it a rat? A bacoon?" Which resembled the raccoons of earth but with spiked tails and much sharper teeth. Funny how the universe might be vast, but certain bottom feeders existed in every culture.

"If it's a rat, then it's a big one," the ensign said.

"Get the inoculation kit ready." They kept a few in engineering at all times because of the rodent problem. Being in space didn't make the rats immune to disease, and humans were highly susceptible.

He stuck his head in the crate, metal hand flexing. It wouldn't be the first time he'd caught a lively bugger. He'd have to make sure he crushed it without spilling any blood. Blood and the silicia didn't mix well.

At first, he didn't see anything, the fluffy leaves filling the space. He began to dig them out, handing them back to the ensigns crowding at his back. He kept pulling them out, wondering if the ensign had imagined movement.

Except there, at the very back in a space it had cleared. A shape. Huddled in a cloak.

A stowaway.

"You. Hiding in the crate. Get out here."

The hood shook, and the body shrank.

"Don't make me drag you out."

Slowly, the hood turned, and he saw straight through the shadows hiding her face to the giant violet eyes inside.

Eyes that widened upon seeing him.

"Who are you?" he barked.

The figure in the cloak didn't reply, and yet he could have sworn he heard someone whisper, *Your destiny*.

THE END.

NEXT: *THE CYBORG'S STOWAWAY*.

Looking for more science fiction romance and space opera? Then visit EveLanglais.com

CPSIA information can be obtained
at www.ICGtesting.com
Printed in the USA
LVOW10s1021140518
577101LV00001B/97/P